YOMI
AND THE **FURY** OF **NINKI NANKA**

THE
ATLANTIC
OCEAN

THE GAMBIA

GAMBIA RIVER

Cape Point Beach

Sukuta

Banjul

Soma

Gunjur

Sibanor

Kalagi

SENEGAL

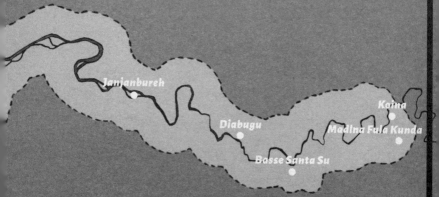

SENEGAL

Janjanbureh

Diabugu

Kaina

Madina Fala Kunda

Basse Santa Su

GUINEA-BISSAU

AFRICA

To Dad, Mum, Yasmin, Mummy and the rest of my family who always supported me. To all my friends who always encouraged me, and to my fellow writers who always inspired me. – D. T.

To my parents, Cynthia and Mark, I will be forever grateful for you helping me follow my dreams. – A. D-B.

LITTLE TIGER
An imprint of Little Tiger Press Limited
1 Coda Studios, 189 Munster Road,
London SW6 6AW

Imported into the EEA by Penguin Random House Ireland,
Morrison Chambers, 32 Nassau Street, Dublin D02 YH68

www.littletiger.co.uk

First published in Great Britain 2023
Text copyright © Davina Tijani, 2023
Illustrations copyright © Adam Douglas-Bagley, 2023

ISBN: 978-1-78895-612-3

The right of Davina Tijani and Adam Douglas-Bagley to be identified as the author and illustrator of this work has been asserted by them in accordance with the Copyright, Designs and Patents Act, 1988.

A CIP catalogue record for this book is available from the British Library.

Printed and bound in the UK.

MIX
Paper | Supporting
responsible forestry
FSC® C171272

The Forest Stewardship Council® (FSC®) is a global, not-for-profit organization dedicated to the promotion of responsible forest management worldwide. FSC defines standards based on agreed principles for responsible forest stewardship that are supported by environmental, social, and economic stakeholders. To learn more, visit www.fsc.org

2 4 6 8 10 9 7 5 3

DAVINA TIJANI
ILLUSTRATED BY ADAM DOUGLAS-BAGLEY

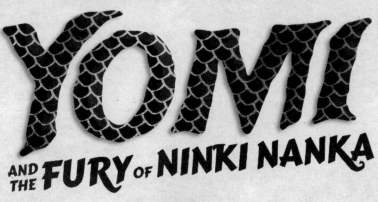

YOMI
AND THE FURY OF NINKI NANKA

LITTLE TIGER
LONDON

CHAPTER 1
THE DRAGON KING

The sky exploded like a supernova. This was no regular storm but one furious at the rest of the world. It was crazy, dangerous ... *exciting!*

"Have you seen this?" Yomi turned eagerly to her younger brother Kayode, who had a toothbrush in his mouth.

"Definitely the worst one since we got to The Gambia," Kayode replied, through the minty foam.

"I wonder what's causing it?"

"As long as those lightning bolts don't fry us, who cares!" Kayode headed back to the bathroom where Yomi could hear him gargling far more energetically than necessary. She wasn't so sure.

Just then their bedroom door opened and

their uncle Olu entered the room. "Have you two brushed your teeth?"

"Yup!" Yomi and Kayode said in unison.

"Good, so time for a story, right?" he offered.

As Yomi guided her long cornrow braids into a green bonnet, she watched Olu quickly divert his eyes to the raging storm outside. He was always watching, always alert.

"Make sure it's a good one, Uncle!" she demanded.

Olu, slightly startled, turned back to his niece and nephew. "A good one?"

"There are so many to choose from!" Kayode dived into bed before making himself comfortable under the covers.

Their uncle grabbed a chair and slotted himself between them. "Hmm..." He stroked his short beard in deep thought. "All right, how about 'Ninki Nanka: the Dragon King.'"

Yomi's eyes widened and she sat up straight in the bed. That was one of her favourites! "Yes! The Dragon King, please!"

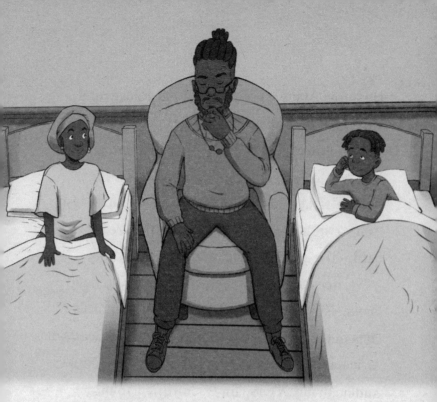

"Many moons ago, during the age of the Mali Empire, enemies would try to cross the Gambia River to invade the empire. Ninki Nanka would spring out of the waters and order the trespassers to leave or face the consequences. All the groups left except for one – *the Lethu*."

Yomi and Kayode were transfixed. Uncle Olu had this way of telling a good story.

"The Lethu were an army of prowlers who had come together to storm The Gambia for its

3

treasures. Made up of mercenaries, thieves and explorers, they all had one thing in common – a lust for power and an obsession with *hunting*. You see, to conquer an empire was a challenge, but to defeat a Sacred Nkara was the ultimate test. And so the stage was set for one of the greatest battles the continent had ever seen."

Stories ran through their family like water and Ninki Nanka often featured in Yomi's grandma's tales of the Nkara – the Sacred and Grand Beasts of Africa. But the idea of people trying to hurt Ninki Nanka, or any Nkara, always horrified Yomi.

"Are the Lethu like Beast Hunters? The people who hunt Nkara?" Yomi had never heard of them before and Olu nodded grimly.

"Whoa! Who won?" Kayode asked.

Their uncle sat back, satisfied. "Ninki Nanka, of course. He defeated them all! And so Mansa Musa, the ruler of the Mali Empire, rewarded him with the title – the Dragon King of The Gambia and Protector of the Gambia River."

"A king." Kayode smiled at the thought of a great

dragon ruling over an entire country.

"Does he wear a crown?" Yomi joked.

"A crown doesn't make a king." Olu laughed. "Ninki Nanka's only goal is to guard the river and its inhabitants, like he's been doing for centuries. The river is the country's bloodline and without Ninki Nanka, well ... let's not think about it."

"Have people seen him?" Yomi asked. There had been a time where Sacred Nkara dominated the land, but that world had now become unrecognizable. Everyone knew Nkara existed but now the creatures preferred to stay out of sight and out of harm's way, especially as there were groups dedicated to hunting them. Of course, some people might be lucky enough to spot one, but whether you lived to tell the tale depended on the Beast.

"Fleeting glimpses of Ninki Nanka here, shadows there. But it is thought he still patrols the river."

"Does he breathe fire?"

"Well—"

"Is there more than one Ninki Nanka?"

"Let me—"

"Is he the strongest Nkara in the world?"

"That's hard to say—"

"Oh! Oh! I know, does he *eat* people?" Kayode's eager-eyed expression changed into one of alarm. "Actually, don't answer that!"

Their uncle took a deep breath. "Ninki Nanka is a water dragon, so no fire. He is the only one left of his kind. His strength? Well, I wouldn't want to face him if he was angry. His fury can shake the world! And, as to whether he would eat you." Olu looked at Kayode's wide eyes and chuckled. "No, you're right. I won't answer that."

"What does he look like again?" Yomi pressed, always wanting to hear this.

"He is huge, with a body like a gigantic crocodile covered in scales. His tail is shaped like a rudder so he can slice through water like a knife. His eyes are green like the jungle and they give him perfect night and underwater vision. He has rows of teeth which mask both a long, forked tongue and glands from where he spurts out his water attacks. He has three horns on his head, four wings and razor-point claws to slash into his enemies." Olu sliced his hands up through the air.

"Great, so now we know to look for him in both the sky *and* water!"

"No, Yomi. *Never* go looking for him. It is no game," their uncle said in a suddenly serious tone. "Anyway, we have other plans while we are here."

Yomi rolled her eyes at that. Olu probably meant work. This was supposed to be a holiday and an important one – after this summer Yomi would be going into Year Six (her last year at school!) and Kayode into Year Four. But so far everything had somehow involved their uncle's Nkara research, without any Nkara! Yomi was just hoping for a bit of fun. A bit of *adventure.*

"It's time for you both to go to bed." Olu turned again towards the storm, thrashing against the glass as if it wanted to break in. "Like this weather, there's already enough against us."

"Uncle?" Yomi looked at Olu and his troubled expression.

"Don't worry about it, Yomi. With my work, some people don't understand what's important but I'm going to make them see sense."

Yomi frowned. Their uncle could be so secretive!

Olu gave both Kayode and Yomi a hug before heading to the door. "Goodnight, you two. You'll need a good sleep before all the exciting things we have planned for tomorrow. You don't get to see a Yarcoss nest every day!" he said before switching off the light and exiting the room.

Kayode was already snoring by the time his head hit his pillow and Yomi threw the covers over her head to block out her brother's annoying sounds. But finally she too soon began to drift off.

Yomi always dreamed of Nkara. Big and small, winged and multi-legged. Hairy, scaled or covered in feathers. Some friendly and others dangerous. Yarcosses, despite their multiple rows of teeth, were known to be gentle to humans when encountered. So when in her dream Yomi entered their nest and reached out her hand to the Nkara, she was horrified when it opened its mouth to yell at her.

"ROOOOOOOAAAAAARRR."

Yomi sat up with a start, her heart beating furiously.

"*What the...?*" Hopping out of bed, she raced to the window. Her palms and nose stuck to the glass as she looked out for something, anything. In the back of her mind she knew that the noise wasn't just in her dream. It sounded like the battle cry of an impossible Beast, the declaration of war against an evil enemy.

She stared hard into the thick black mist and watched as the charcoal clouds twisted then expanded as though invisible hands were squeezing them like sponges.

Then there was a flash of a tail, a hint of a fin, and a glimpse of large wings zipping between the thunderclouds at supersonic speed.

"No, it can't be..." Yomi rubbed her eyes, in case they were playing tricks on her. What she had seen matched their uncle's description. Only *bigger*! The size of a whale. "It's Ninki Nanka!"

But what she also saw was something racing – or *chasing* – right behind it.

A white mist, flying through the air, tying itself around the fleeing creature before a murky fog swallowed the entire scene and they disappeared from sight!

"Kay!" Yomi had to stifle her shout.

She ran over and shook her brother by the shoulders, but even that didn't wake him. Kayode could sleep through an earthquake! There was only one thing for it. Yomi ran to the bathroom and returned a moment later with a cup of freezing water. At first, she sprinkled a few drops on his face.

Kayode twitched his nose.

She tried again.

Dreamily, he wiped his face.

"Gah!" Yomi groaned, and threw the entire cup of water over her brother.

"Blurggh!" Kayode stared at his sister, saw the cup and then noted the guilty expression on her face. "What is *wrong* with you?" he spluttered.

"I saw Ninki Nanka in the sky."

"Who goes throwing water in people's faces when... Wait, you saw the Dra—?"

Yomi slapped her hand over Kayode's mouth before he woke the entire hotel.

"Don't let everyone hear you," she hushed, staring at the bedroom door. The last thing she wanted was for their uncle to rush in.

"I can't believe you didn't wake me!"

Yomi looked at her brother – was he being serious?

"Do you know how *rare* it is to see a Nkara? A Sacred or even a Grand?" Kayode's voice was now so high, Yomi thought only dogs could hear him! But she understood his excitement. The stories were absolutely, definitely all *true*.

"I think he was in trouble." Yomi sounded concerned. Scared even. And if his sister was scared then Kayode definitely was too.

"Why? What happened?"

"I don't know. He was being chased, though. Something or someone wanted to hurt him, or they already had."

"Or maybe the thunder hit him and he was actually tumbling from the sky." As soon as Kayode finished speaking he shook his head. He'd only managed to frighten himself!

The fast tap of feet coming up the corridor towards their bedroom cut their conversation short. Just as they jumped back into their beds, their uncle gently opened the door to check if they were asleep. He was on his phone and they could just make out his whispers.

"A new assignment?" Olu asked in his quietest voice. "Ninki Nanka?" He wasn't giving much away and with one final glance at the children, he closed the door and walked off.

Waiting just enough time to be sure their uncle was at a safe distance, Yomi quietly padded over to the door, followed closely by Kayode. Opening it a little, they could see Olu had stopped halfway down the corridor.

"A party at Madam Ngom's house for *them*." Their uncle sighed.

Yomi looked back at Kayode, who simply shrugged. Who was Madam Ngom?

"I refuse to attend if they are there," Olu continued. "This truce is ridiculous and I told everyone how I felt about the deal. It's only a matter of time before they cross the line." He went silent for a few moments to listen to the response.

"I will think about it. I have my family with me and I'd rather steer clear of any parties," he said dismissively, then waited again. "OK. Goodnight." For just a moment Olu stood staring at the phone. With another heavy sigh, he carried on down the corridor back to his room.

"We're going to figure this out," Yomi said.

"Figure what out?"

"What's going on with Ninki Nanka, obviously!"

"No." Kayode shook his head profusely. "No. No. No! I don't want to get wrapped up with a dragon."

"Too late." Yomi grinned. "So you better sleep good tonight. Tomorrow we need to keep our eyes wide open."

CHAPTER 2

THE BEAST HUNTERS' GUILD

The golden sun hung high in the sky, its intense heat beating down on the roads of The Gambia's capital city, Banjul. Yomi's brown skin glowed hot and sweaty yet all she could think of was Ninki Nanka. Had it been a dream? Their uncle had said as much when she told him at breakfast what she'd seen.

"Nkara are the strongest Beasts in the world. They don't get chased by mist," he'd told her. "Forget about it." But she couldn't. Yomi knew what she had seen.

Olu was a Nkara researcher for the Mikosi Institute, and lectured at universities all over the world on African Studies. His talk at the university this morning had overrun (unsurprisingly), delaying their trip to the Yarcoss nest by a few hours. Now they wouldn't arrive until after midday, when the sun was at its strongest. Yomi poked her head out of the car window, letting the light wind whip through her hair as she looked out at the city.

Yellow taxis with green stripes were interspersed with packed buses, snazzy 4x4s and colourful bikes. People were dressed in broad and bright mixes of traditional and Western clothing. Under the umbrella-hooded stalls lining the pavements, street traders were selling goods like food and clothes. All the buildings were low-rise, painted in creamy browns and housed the shops and mosques of the city.

"We'll soon be at Cape Point beach. Yarcosses are known to live in huge colonies but they've left their nest so something major must have happened," their uncle noted.

"So they aren't actually going to be there?" Yomi mumbled. She couldn't see the point of going somewhere if the Nkara had all left. She wanted to see one *so* badly.

"I'm going to find a nice palm tree and build the biggest sandcastle ever!" Kayode vowed, raising his head up from the latest issue of Arabella Carter, his favourite comic book series. Yomi smiled at her brother's enthusiasm, but with an enormous chunk of the day already gone, Yomi doubted they'd have time for that.

Olu turned the car on to another road. "I'm sorry, Yomi. But as the nest isn't going to be as exciting as you'd hoped, maybe we could visit Mansa's Stone too."

"What's Mansa's Stone?" Kayode asked.

"A monument built by Mansa Musa after the Lethu were defeated," Olu answered.

Ever since their parents had agreed they could spend the summer holidays with their uncle, he had promised them a trip of a lifetime. Olu had always taken them to cool places in London. So far, though, despite their uncle's attempts to make his research fun, it had proved quite boring – apart from the dragon in the sky, of course!

"Uncle, about what I saw in the sky last night," Yomi said, picking up their discussion from earlier. "I think Ninki Nanka is—"

A tap on the car window cut her sentence short. A young man dressed in an indigo shirt and black trousers was riding a motorbike alongside the car. He held up a black envelope with a golden 'S' in the centre. Yomi looked at their uncle. He didn't seem to be that surprised by the man's presence.

Olu pulled over and parked the car on the roadside. The motorcyclist quickly followed and once their uncle had wound down the window, the man handed him the letter.

"From Madam Ngom. You are to read it now." And with his message delivered, the stranger sped off, zipping between cars before disappearing.

"What is it, Uncle?" Kayode asked, exchanging confused glances with Yomi.

"How did that man know where we were?" said Yomi.

Olu didn't answer. His face now held a disgruntled expression as he read the letter.

"I need to call someone, so please can you be quiet, just for a moment?" Their uncle punched in a number on his phone. Using the hands-free mode, he started up the car again and Yomi guessed they were no longer going to the beach.

"Salaam Alaikum, Na nga def?" Olu said in a stern voice. Was he speaking Wolof? That was one of The Gambia's most spoken languages. The person (a woman, Yomi thought) on the other end sounded harsh. Yomi and Kayode watched as Olu's face scrunched further as the conversation went on. "Madam Ngom, I don't want to argue with you," he snapped in English before taking a deep breath and calming himself. "I will go there now, madam," he said, before ending the call.

Kayode groaned his disappointment while Yomi couldn't even feel sad. The image of Ninki Nanka getting swallowed up was all she could think about. When the car came to a stop in traffic, their uncle looked back at them with an apologetic smile. "I'm so sorry. There's been a change of plan. One last stop, OK?" And with no further explanation, he quickly turned the car in the opposite direction.

Yomi took in everything around them as they drove on. They had moved further away from the metropolis of Banjul and were seemingly headed into the middle of nowhere.

Despite being surrounded by leafy nature she couldn't help but feel the area was empty. Forgotten even. There was barely a sound, as if the wildlife had been forced from their posts, and the baobab trees, bamboo and shrubs were completely overgrown. So much so it was no surprise that Yomi and Kayode nearly missed the enormous cave!

Olu had clearly been here before, however, and judging by the sour look on his face, he wasn't impressed to be back.

"Where are we?" Kayode asked.

"The Beast Hunters' Guild. Let's go." Olu got out of the car and marched towards the cave's entrance. After a moment's hesitation, Yomi and Kayode quickly followed suit, chasing after their uncle with a host of questions.

"The hunters have a guild?"

"Are they here now?" Kayode asked, and Yomi could hear the concern in his voice.

"They've gone. Trust me, we wouldn't have got this close if they were and I wouldn't have brought you here," Olu answered. "You know there are still hunters all around the world searching for Nkara?"

Yomi and Kay nodded.

"But why?" Kayode looked confused.

"Some do it for the challenge, some for the thrill, and some for the glory. But they all hunt for the victory – the triumph of man over Beast."

"So why are we here now?" Yomi asked.

"To pick up some items they left behind. They left in a rush."

As they stood at the entrance, Yomi took in several vans within the perimeter, all being loaded with cargo. Then she noted the plaque right above the entrance:

BEAST HUNTERS' GUILD

THE HUNT NEVER ENDS:
POWER | DOMINATION | PRIDE | CONTROL

As Yomi read the words in front of her, several questions came to mind. *Who were these people? How was Uncle Olu involved? Did this have anything to do with what she'd seen last night?*

Kayode and Yomi followed their uncle, coming to a huge stop when they saw what was inside the cave.

"Wow!" said Kayode, and Yomi couldn't agree more.

Steel tubes, brass chains and mahogany pillars had been embedded deep into the cavern's rock to strike a fearsome appearance. Paintings of Nkara hung from the rock slabs and small lanterns were fixed in the walls. Abstract circles had been chiselled out to form windows, allowing the sunlight to illuminate everything. The building resembled a museum, minus the actual artefacts.

All the display cabinets were completely

empty, their windowpanes smashed, and even the description plaques had been carved out of existence.

They passed the statue of a muscular man who must have been at least seven feet tall, and who held an ida sword and a long rifle. Yomi shivered at the figure's bloodthirsty glare.

All around them people wearing the same indigo uniforms as the motorcyclist from earlier hurriedly sifted through and cleared the debris. Olu waved and spoke briefly with those they bumped into.

"Olusola!" A man around the same age as their uncle approached them.

A huge grin took over Olu's face as he and the stranger hugged. The man then smiled at Yomi and Kayode.

"Your niece and nephew, Olu?" He shook both of their hands.

"That's right. My older brother's children," Olu explained.

"Yemi's kids! At last we meet," the man said excitedly. "Introducing them to the family business?"

Olu gave him a playful punch. "Kind of... Within reason."

"Remind me of your names?" the man asked them.

"Yomi."

"I'm Kayode."

"Nice to meet you. My name is Daba Toure. I've known Olu and your father for a *long* time. Since we were your age actually—"

"Do we know where the Guild went?" Olu interrupted, looking around at all the empty displays.

"Probably somewhere far away from Banjul. They mobilize quick, I'll give them that."

"So, Soma, Janjanbureh, or maybe Kalagi?" Olu listed off other Gambian cities.

"Not sure yet. It's not as empty as it seems, though, they didn't quite take everything. So far we've found weapon crafters, jetpacks, shadow masks, battle gauntlets and some other hunting tools."

"A jetpack?" Yomi asked excitedly. "Can I use it?"

"No," Olu answered.

Daba smiled at her and shrugged his shoulders.

"Can I at least wear the shadow mask?" Kayode asked.

"*No*," Olu answered again, before turning back to Daba who gave them another guilty smile.

"We haven't found any specimens, so clearly they weren't prepared to leave those behind." Daba handed over a group of old books of different lengths. "And they left these. Madam Ngom wants them."

As Olu flicked through the titles, Yomi tried to take in the names: *Yinza: Descendants of the Moon; Beast Riddles* and *Guide to Nkara Habitats.*

"Anything on the computers?" Olu questioned.

"All wiped." Daba lowered his voice before continuing. "The Biji Pact has been broken. They must have known we would notice the disturbances in protected areas, which have been reported all over the continent."

"They never intended to follow the rules," Olu hissed angrily.

"And there's something else," Daba continued.

"What?" Olu probed.

"Something has happened to Ninki Nanka."

"I saw him disappear in the sky," Yomi spoke up.

"A white mist swallowed him," Kayode added.

"Yomi, I told you that was not possible. The only thing which can defeat a Nkara is Yi—" Olu's words trailed off as if he'd realized something, and he gave his friend a hard stare.

"But to trap a Nkara, to trap Ninki Nanka!" Daba uttered the last words quietly.

"They *are* using it. I knew it, the hunters..." Olu declared.

"Using what? Knew what?" Yomi questioned but

their uncle refused to answer and started speaking in Wolof to Daba. The only words Yomi could understand were Ninki Nanka, magic and Beast Hunters. Daba glanced at Yomi and Kayode, then guided their uncle to the other side of the room for more privacy.

"These guys don't sound good, Kay. And now magic is involved?" Yomi shook her head. "Hunting. Ugh."

"But why?" Kayode asked. "Everyone knows that if – and it's a very big IF – you see these creatures, you don't stay and play, you run! I mean, I know Uncle researches Beasts and everything but Beast Hunters, secret cave museums... What is going on!" he complained. "We should be on the beach, building sandcastles!"

"Kay, that's not going to help us find out what happened to Ninki Nanka. Look, we're right here in the Beast Hunters' headquarters and *still* Uncle is not telling us everything."

"Maybe to protect us. Because, you know, that's what uncles are *supposed* to do."

"Well, I don't want protection from the truth! I want to find Ninki Nanka," Yomi announced, grabbing her brother. "And since no one is telling us anything, we must get the answers ourselves."

"Yomi!" Kayode sighed. "One day you're going to get us into trouble that we can't get out of."

CHAPTER 3

DISCOVERY OF BONES

Yomi needed a plan to find Ninki Nanka and a place to think through everything they had learned so far. Annoyingly it wasn't a lot! The fact that magic was involved in Ninki Nanka's disappearance made her even more eager to learn the truth.

Seeing how focused everyone was on their work, Yomi decided to use the opportunity to look around. She and Kayode kept moving until they found a room with no one inside.

Shiny shards of metal, worryingly resembling teeth, were moulded into its rock walls. As the sun shone through the single window, the light reflected off the fragments, creating a metallic flush of neon-rainbow colours around the room.

"Is it just me or is it really cold in here?" Kayode said out loud.

Yomi nodded. An icy tingle ran up from her toes as she looked around for the source of the sudden dip in temperature. It was completely at odds with the heat outside.

"I've never seen a cave like this before." Kayode spun round.

"You haven't been in a cave before full stop," Yomi pointed out.

"I don't need to have been in a cave to know this is weird!" Kayode flung his hands at the various colours dancing across the walls.

Yomi walked over to the empty bookcases and started feeling along the upper shelves.

"What are you looking for?" Kayode asked.

"Maybe a clue. I think the hunters are somehow involved in Ninki Nanka's disappearance... Nothing there," Yomi huffed.

"Move over," Kayode chimed.

"What?"

"Watch this." Kayode started tapping all over the bookcase while Yomi watched on in confusion. Suddenly a secret compartment sprung open, revealing a tatty scroll.

"How did you...?"

"Arabella Carter, volume twenty-three," Kayode said with a smug smile.

"Which one is that?"

"When she was in Venezuela looking for the Bogora Papyrus," Kayode said as he unravelled the scroll. At the top of the page there was a symbol of two crossed spears and a Beast's head roaring at the reader.

BEAST HUNTERS' GUILD CHARTER

THE GUIDELINES IN THIS DOCUMENT MUST BE FOLLOWED ACROSS THE CONTINENT. ADDITIONAL REGIONAL RULES ARE APPLICABLE.

The Beast Hunters' Guild remains dedicated to its central goal — the elimination of power held by Nkara, by whatever means.

ALL MEMBERS MUST ADHERE TO THE FOLLOWING RULES:

1.
The Guild always comes first. No exceptions, no excuses.

2.
Hunters may be members of different factions within the Guild i.e. Association of Spirit Catchers, Mutant Squad, Troll Hunters, Flying Union and Ancient Battalion.

3.
Beast ownership is only allowed with the permission of senior Guild members.

4.
No unsanctioned hunts. Severe punishment will befall anyone who does.

5.
An attack against a Guild member is an attack against the entire Beast Hunters' Guild. Any enemy of the Guild must be eliminated.

6.
Yinza is our weapon. Use is encouraged.

7.
Hunters must never harm another Guild member. To do so means punishment of death.

Guild Structure

1.
Beast Prime: The sole leader of the Guild. Their authority is not questioned, their rule is absolute. All decisions and actions of the Guild are ultimately made by them.

2.
Beast Masters: Advisors of the Beast Prime. Beast Masters can only be appointed by the Beast Prime.

3.
Beast Leader: Leaders of a hunt. They also train and guide apprentices. To become a Beast Leader, an individual must have completed at least fifty hunts.

4.
Beast Hunter: Once a member has taken part in one hunt, they are given the title of Beast Hunter.

5.
Apprentice Beast Hunter: All new members of the Beast Hunters' Guild are assigned this title. You are students of the Guild.

The hunt will not end until all Sacred Nkara are exterminated, only then will the balance of power for humans over Beasts be restored. This is _our_ world.

"I wonder what *Yinza* means. It was mentioned on one of the books Uncle Daba gave Uncle Olu."

"Who cares? These people are crazy!" Kayode shattered Yomi's careful deliberation. "How can they even believe that Beasts are less powerful than us?"

"Yes, and now we've seen this, there's no way you can think they didn't take Ninki Nanka." Yomi rolled up the scroll and tucked it into her backpack.

"Shouldn't we give it to Uncle? Maybe it could help him."

"It can help *us*, Kay." Olu's secrecy was bothering Yomi. Why bring them here, only to keep them in the dark? Well, *she* could keep secrets too.

Kayode shook his head. Carefully stepping over the broken glass, he suddenly crouched down to pick up a piece of metal sitting among the shards. He examined it more closely. It was the size of a pen, with a jagged point like a key, and shone like copper, despite being as hard as steel.

"What's that?" Yomi enquired.

"A lock pick I think." Kayode held it up to the light.

"It could come in useful!"

Yomi nodded her head. She continued to look on the floor in case there was anything else. "No way!"

"What? *What?*" Kayode spun round. There was a square indentation in the ground.

"D'you reckon it's a..." The siblings looked at each other excitedly.

"Trapdoor!" they said together.

With care, they shifted everything out of the way and found the small handle cleverly hidden within the floor design. They pulled the latch and as the door opened, a gust of icy dust and dirt attacked them.

"That's disgusting!" Kayode choked, frantically waving his hand in front of his face.

"So this is where the cold came from." Yomi coughed, but all thoughts of old dirt left her mind when the air cleared.

She could see the first rung of a ladder and down the sides were the smallest of lights, guiding them into what was an unnervingly deep, dark hole.

Yomi picked up a piece of glass and threw it

down, waiting to hear it smash.

They stood and, eventually ... PLINK! Yup, it was a very deep hole.

"Let's go down and look! We might find clues about where they're keeping Ninki Nanka," Yomi said. And it was only when Kayode looked over to his sister in disbelief that he realized she'd already begun descending into the gloom, one step at a time.

"Yomi!" Kayode shouted after her.

"Come on." Her voice echoed back up. Kayode groaned and followed his sister down.

As she climbed, Yomi realized that the bulbs were actually coming from glow worms trapped within the glass seals.

"Hey, check out the lights!" she called up to her brother. Kayode stopped to examine one of the critters. It looked back at him with a disturbingly curious expression. But just as Kayode was about to say "cool!", the insect bared its razor-sharp teeth and emitted a hideous screech before ramming itself into the glass.

"ARGH! Go, Yomi, go go go!" shouted Kayode as he lost his footing, falling down the ladder and taking Yomi with him. They landed with an unceremonious thump next to each other.

"Ow, Kay! What were you doing?"

"Did you see that? It was about to rip off my head!"

"The worm?"

"*Yes*, the worm. It was a mutant!"

Yomi picked herself up from the ground and followed the flicker of a glow into the underground chamber. Kayode pulled himself to his feet and raced after her.

"I wonder how far this place stretches on for?" Yomi thought out loud.

"Do you think Ninki Nanka is being kept down he— Oof!" Kayode collided into Yomi's back and then realized what had caught her attention.

Along the back walls, there were bones, fossils, unusual-coloured eggs, hair, horns, fur, teeth, claws, talons, feathers and scales, all stored in jars.

"Whoa, this is gross!" said Kayode, pointing at the severed arm of a giant octopus.

"And cruel." Beside Yomi stood the full skeleton of a Nkara. The bones were black, extra elongated, and the tail bone was over a metre long. Its jawbone was open wide enough to see all the rows of teeth.

"Yomi, is that a..." Kayode whispered.

"It's a Yarcoss," she finished. "Now we know why they left their nest." Yomi shook her head, fear radiating through her body.

She stepped closer, hearing her grandma's words in her head. *To hunt Nkara is one of the cruellest of crimes.* Yomi could almost sense the tremor of terror captured in the empty sockets of its skull.

She tentatively rubbed her fingers along its curved wing bones and gasped. "The bones are still warm."

"Will they do this to Ninki Nanka?" Kayode asked.

"I don't know. I mean, no. No, we can't let that happen. We have to stop them."

Suddenly, shouts from above caught their attention.

"Yomi, Kayode, are you down there?"

"Yes, Uncle." Yomi looked guiltily at her brother.

"What are you doing?" Olu demanded.

"There are bones and all sorts down here," Kayode replied.

There was a swift exchange of hushed words.

"Both of you, up here. Now!"

They didn't hang around and quickly made their way back to the ladder, but not before Yomi had grabbed the first specimen jar she could.

"See?" Yomi handed their uncle the jar containing a claw. Olu lifted it to the light while Daba and several others who had since crowded round made their way down to the chamber.

"Uncle, what's going on?" Kayode whispered when he saw the sick look on Olu's face.

"You weren't supposed to see this."

"We can help, though. I want to protect the Nkara, just like you," Yomi declared.

"No!"

Yomi stepped back but remained determined. "The Guild used magic to take Ninki Nanka, didn't they?"

Olu froze. "How could

47

you know..." He shook his head before continuing. "I'm sorry, but as you've guessed, the beach is off. This is much worse than I thought."

For the first time since they arrived, Yomi wasn't bothered about not having fun. She made a silent vow. She was going to find Ninki Nanka and rescue the dragon from whatever danger had wrapped itself around him that stormy night.

CHAPTER 4

THE MYSTERIOUS DOOR

After a long, silent journey, the trio finally came to a halt outside a grand detached mansion. Held up by a number of pillars, the villa had several balconies and a huge black and gold gate at the entrance to the estate. They waited a few long moments before the gate eventually swung open.

"So *who* exactly are we coming to stay with?" Yomi asked.

"My mentor. Her name is Binta Ngom. She's an important person here in The Gambia," Olu explained.

"Do you know her from work?" Kayode said. "You and Uncle Daba, do you all work together?"

"Something like that." Olu kept his eyes on

the house.

"So we should call her Aunty Binta?" Yomi asked carefully.

"Exactly." Their uncle parked the car.

One moment they were in some kind of Nkara mausoleum, now they were at some random woman's house and *still* their uncle hadn't told them what was going on or let them help. Yomi tried to swallow her frustration.

A moment later the front door opened and an older woman stepped out, waving at them enthusiastically. She reminded Yomi of her grandma, especially as she was wrapped in a sun-drenched yellow kaftan – her grandma's favourite colour.

"Welcome!" Aunty Binta said with a lively voice. She took them into her arms to give each a big hug. "I haven't seen either of you since you were little, when Adeyemi and Stéphanie brought you to my house in London. Do you remember?"

At the mention of their parents' names, Yomi and Kayode exchanged a look.

"I remember," Olu replied. Yomi didn't. She didn't

recognize this lady at all. Why had
their uncle not mentioned this
before bringing them here?
Aunty Binta was all smiles and
warmth with them, but Yomi
couldn't miss the icy atmosphere
that encircled the grown-ups.

"Hello, Olu," Aunty Binta finally addressed him directly.

"Madam Ngom, it's been too long."

"Yes, too long. Come. Come inside, let me show Yomi and Kayode around. You've arrived with plenty of time before the party tonight."

Aunty Binta introduced them to her housekeeper. "Anything you children need, ask Mrs Sanyang and she will see to it."

As Aunty Binta continued the grand tour, Yomi was amazed. She slowly spun round trying to take everything in and couldn't help feel that Aunty Binta's home was more like a palace.

"Oh my days – have you seen that swimming pool?" Kayode grabbed Yomi in excitement.

"Jump in whenever you want." Aunty Binta chuckled.

"I will." Kayode turned to Yomi. "I mean, *we* will. Won't we?"

Yomi rolled her eyes. How could her brother be so easily distracted? Especially after what they had seen at the Beast Hunters' Guild. How could he forget about Ninki Nanka? And now, here they were, with a woman who knew their parents but who Uncle Olu didn't seem to like. A stream of questions was running through her mind and all Kayode could think about was splashing in a pool!

They went from room to room, including a games room with everything from arcade machines and tabletop games to a conservatory, which seemed to be growing a jungle. Yet while Aunty Binta had taken them seemingly through every single doorway, there was one she made no effort to even stop by. Naturally, Yomi was curious. How could she not be? The dark purple door was ornately engraved with coils and at its centre was a capital 'S', exactly like the one on the envelope Uncle Olu had received earlier that day.

But the moment to question what was in there disappeared as Aunty Binta moved on to the next door. It was a magnificent library, containing bookcases as tall as skyscrapers, filled with enough books for Yomi to read for eternity.

Yomi looked up towards the ceiling, where the library took on a circular shape, with an observation level high above the ground only accessible by a couple of ladders Yomi couldn't wait to climb up.

"You are most welcome to come to the library any time you want." Aunty Binta touched Yomi's shoulder. "My husband would get lost in here for hours... Right, now let me show you to your bedrooms."

She guided them down a series of wide and winding corridors. The place never seemed to end!

"How big is the house, Aunty?" Kayode asked.

"Three floors – my late husband always wanted more space for our work."

What was their work exactly? Yomi wondered.

At last, Aunty Binta led them to a room with ochre-yellow walls and mahogany furniture. There was a king-sized bed with a canopy for each of them.

"Olu, you can have the room next door."

Their uncle thanked her, picking up his suitcases and heading into his new temporary accommodation.

Aunty Binta turned back to Yomi and Kayode. "The party starts in a few hours, so relax until then. It will be a night to remember as we are expecting some special visitors," she said before swiftly departing.

As soon as their door clicked shut, Kayode flew around their new space. He looked through the wardrobes before cartwheeling on the free floor space, while Yomi pondered the party and who the *special visitors* could be.

"This is awesome!" Kayode exploded.

Yomi agreed but why did they leave their hotel so abruptly? It must be to do with Ninki Nanka, Yomi thought, but could Aunty Binta be trusted? This must be the party Uncle didn't want to go to. But *why* didn't he want to go?

"What do you think about Aunty Binta?" she asked Kayode.

"She's putting us up in *style*!" Keen to test the bed, Kayode jumped up and fell with a delighted, gentle thud.

"I think we need to keep an eye on her," Yomi

concluded. There was no doubt that Aunty Binta had been welcoming, but while Olu was wary, she was determined to be as well.

Kayode sighed happily. "We will sleep well tonight!"

"*You* can sleep well anywhere. The end of the world could be happening, all the Sacred Nkara on the planet could go to war against humans and you would still manage to snore your way thro—"

Before she could finish her sentence, a pillow smacked her in the face and all she could hear was Kayode's cheeky laughter.

CHAPTER 5

MADAM NGOM'S PARTY

Yomi had made a plan. If there was to be a grand party, it was an opportunity to get more information.

The entire house had been decorated with gold balloons and silver ribbons, which dangled from the ceiling and walls. A DJ was stationed at the corner of the reception room with his booming speakers controlling the vibe. The appetizing smells of the buffet table drew Yomi across the room. Different-coloured rice and meat dishes like benachi, domoda and chicken yassa were waiting. Once she'd found out something interesting, she would treat herself to a heaped plate of it all as a reward. In the meantime, since she couldn't investigate on an empty stomach,

Yomi took one dessert – chakery topped with slices of fruit. She looked around for Kayode and found him ripping up the dance floor with killer moves to his favourite Afrobeats song.

Yomi walked through to the main living room where everyone was dressed in gorgeous African attire. Most wore long flowing kaftans, the women adorned with embroidered headdresses tightly wound around their heads. Not willing to be outdressed, Yomi's ankara sparkled like dark blue diamonds while Kayode looked smart in his purple dashiki.

"Having a good time?" Aunty Binta materialized by Yomi's side, sipping her drink.

She caught Yomi completely off guard. "Y-yes, thank you."

"Good. You know, I'm happy you are here with your uncle." Aunty Binta smiled.

"Does he work with you?" Yomi asked.

"Yes. I met him when he was a student and I was his teacher. Now we work together, but in a *special* way. Olu is an expert on everything. African history,

African culture, and of course Nkara. I invited him
to give the talks here in The Gambia."

"Have you seen one before?" Yomi put down her
dessert bowl.

"Seen what?" Aunty Binta replied.

"A Sacred Nkara."

"Once or twice."

"What about Ninki Nanka?" Yomi questioned.

"I saw him once, many years ago. I heard you saw him too." Aunty Binta flipped the questioning round and even though her words were delivered softly, they sounded sharp.

"I saw him get snatched away by something powerful," Yomi replied.

"Don't worry. We have it under control. If Ninki Nanka is truly missing we will find him."

"You mean Uncle Olu and all the people we saw at the Beast Hunters' Guild?" Yomi asked.

But before Yomi could get an answer, another guest had whisked Aunty Binta away. She went to see if she could get anything more out of their uncle. "Is this Aunty Binta's birthday party?" she asked him.

"What? No, her birthday is in January." Olu paused for a moment. "This is a reunion of old friends, of sorts."

"Why don't you want to be here?" she asked, noticing his scowling face.

"Ah, Yomi." Olu looked at his niece and shook his head as though trying to rid his mind of something. "I'm sorry if I've been in a bad mood." He leaned down to hug her. "I want you to have a good holiday with me and not worry about a thing."

Yomi knew that was impossible!

"But you've been kind of angry since we left the Beast Hunters' headquarters," she remarked.

"It's hard when you disagree with those you

respect..." Olu stopped himself. "Are you enjoying the party?" He changed the subject, sipping from his glass.

"Yeah, I guess. Kay is liking it more." Yomi looked over to see her brother impressing everyone as he ruled the dance floor. "At least he's not embarrassing us!"

Olu burst out laughing, making Yomi smile. Then Uncle Daba appeared next to Olu and the pair started chatting back and forth in Wolof. Yomi wondered what their plans were for tomorrow. Just as she was about to ask, a series of gasps followed by the music going dead stopped her.

Some new guests had arrived. They were formidably dressed, wearing a heavy amount of sharp metal sewn into their bright red and orange kaftans. It was as if they were going into battle. Among the new cohort of men and women, Yomi found her attention drawn to the youngest of the group. He was her age, wearing an ocean-blue kaftan, and his curls of hair were the colour of freshly fallen snow.

Yomi had never seen a party's mood turn

so quickly. Aunty Binta walked towards the new guests but the boy sauntered ahead of the group, getting to her first, his hands holding out a gift.

"My dad cannot come, so he sent me instead." He gave a smarmy smile and handed over the present.

Hesitantly, Aunty Binta accepted. "Thank you, Hadim. I'm sure he had his reasons."

As Aunty Binta shook hands with each of the newly arrived party, Yomi couldn't ignore the furious glare on Uncle Olu's face before he stormed towards them.

"Who are they?" Yomi asked Uncle Daba.

"Beasts Hunters," Daba answered ominously and Yomi gasped.

This doesn't make any sense, she thought. *Why would Aunty Binta invite hunters to her party?* She turned her attention back to the commotion their uncle was now causing.

"So you didn't do anything?" Olu smirked.

"You know that even we respect the balance the King provides along the river," the tallest hunter replied.

"*I* know the Beast Prime doesn't care about anything but the hunt," Olu replied.

A woman hunter flashed her teeth at him. "The Prime's will is *our* law but we had nothing to do with Ninki Nanka."

"This has his hands all over it!" their uncle bit out just as Aunty Binta stood in front of him. Yomi guessed

she didn't want the argument escalating.

"The Beast Prime... My dad isn't involved," Hadim spoke up and Olu stared daggers at him.

"I think all hunters are liars, especially your father," Olu replied before walking off.

Aunty Binta looked embarrassed. "Ah, Yomi. Kayode. Please take Hadim and go explore outside."

Yomi led the way and Hadim calmly stepped in between her and Kayode as they walked. She could tell Kayode was nervous around the unknown boy; so was she. Was he a hunter too?

Hadim didn't say anything as they went to an enormous grove filled with African rosewood trees. Suddenly the young hunter stopped, looked up at the tree in front of him and began to climb, giving them a quick smirk as if challenging them.

"Isn't that a bad idea?" Yomi asked.

"Only if you can't do it." Hadim hoisted himself up.

Unwilling to lose face, Yomi followed him while Kayode rolled his eyes and begrudgingly followed them into the higher branches.

"You ever seen a Nkara?" Hadim leaned back into

the tree trunk and put his
hands behind his head.

*What a weird way to start
a conversation*, Yomi thought.
"I saw Ninki Nanka," she said,
then taking note of Hadim's
furrowed eyebrows,
suddenly wished she
hadn't said anything.

"You're lying!"
"Why would I do that?"
"Well, how many Nkara have
you seen then?" Kayode jumped in.

"Loads but not as many as my dad, obviously. He's the greatest Beast Hunter who ever lived, everyone says so. That's why he's Prime."

"So why isn't he here?"

"He's hunting Mutants."

"Mutants like Nkara?" Kayode asked.

"Yeah," Hadim answered. Yomi didn't quite understand it. If Hadim's dad was Beast Prime then surely he would have been there when Ninki Nanka was taken.

"So why are you hunters here at this party? Don't you have your own?" Yomi asked.

"I don't really know. Something about peace between us, like that's going to work!" He laughed. "So, where are your parents?"

"We're here with our uncle Olu."

"Le grossier." Hadim called Olu rude in French.

"Il n'est pas impoli," Kayode replied, defending their uncle. Hadim looked taken aback.

"*You* are being rude," Yomi added.

They all sat awkwardly.

"If you are a hunter, you must know a lot about

Nkara..." Yomi began.

"Nkara have existed since the world began, unfortunately for humans but good for hunters."

"What about Ninki Nanka?" Yomi pushed, keen to learn as much as she could from Hadim.

"Ninki Nanka was born from the Gambia River, unlike most dragons that are born on land. He doesn't leave it very often and being away from it isn't good for him." Yomi and Kayode exchanged a worried look until Hadim spoke again. "Since you like questions, let me ask one."

"Go on," Kayode replied.

"You ever heard of a Mezamorphi?" Hadim asked as the siblings shook their heads. "It means shapeshifter – they can change form," Hadim explained. "They know things, things other people don't know and I hear there are some in The Gambia. I heard there are some on the river right now."

Yomi didn't know what to say to this new information but she let Hadim keep talking, knowing she could learn more.

"And my dad says they're not like Ninki Nanka or the other Nkara. They can become like us and then become the enemy. He admires that sort of power. You know what else he told me..." He leaned in closer to Yomi. "Some magic can change the world and some can destroy it."

CHAPTER 6
SECRET
SOCIETY

The sounds of wheels rumbling and engines dying pulled Yomi out of her sleep. She looked at her bedside clock: 1:53 a.m. The party had wrapped up not too long after their conversation with Hadim, with the hunters leaving immediately.

Back in their room, Yomi was amazed she had fallen asleep with all this new information buzzing in her head. Ninki Nanka, hunters, the Gambia River, Mezamorphi...

Yomi moved towards the window and edged the curtains open to see what was going on. There were cars parked at the front of the house, with people from the party and some new faces being greeted by Aunty Binta and Uncle Olu. Why were they all out there so late?

Yomi quickly stepped back from the window and went to shake Kayode awake. This time he sat bolt upright.

"What! What? What is it?"

Grabbing Kayode's arm, Yomi pulled him out of bed and led him out of the room.

"Yomi?" Kayode whispered. "Where are we—?"

Yomi turned and pressed a finger to her lips. They tiptoed down the corridor, careful not to make a noise. Yomi strained her ears, hoping for some clues. Were the people in the house? Still outside? Or somewhere else on the grounds? This was all so weird! And then Yomi thought of the door marked with the ornate 'S'. She couldn't help but feel this was connected to Ninki Nanka.

Going through the smaller living room and cutting across the conservatory, they came to the 'S' door. It was slightly ajar, the light from inside spilling out into the corridor, inviting them to come closer.

"We have to go inside," Yomi whispered.

"Do we, though?" Kayode replied before reluctantly following her into the room.

Inside, the room was a lot smaller than Yomi had expected. "Is this it? Is this all you wanted to see?" Kayode complained impatiently.

"Let's look around."

"Yomi, there's barely anything in here!"

In the middle of the room sat a round mahogany table and around it, ten golden chairs. In front of each place on the table was a sheet of headed paper emblazoned with dark bold lettering.

Yomi picked up one of the pieces of paper

"*The S.B.L.: One World for All*. What's that about?" asked Kayode, reading over her shoulder.

Before Yomi could answer, the murmur of voices in the corridor made them freeze.

"They're getting closer." Kayode panicked. "Yomi, they're coming in here." He grabbed her arm.

"Calm down." Yomi searched the room for somewhere to hide – there weren't many options!

"The closet. Get in." She pointed at a large cabinet, pressed up against the back wall of the room. Kayode didn't have much choice, Yomi pushed him forwards and then jumped in beside him, closing the door behind them.

As the chattering voices approached, Yomi and Kayode took a keyhole each and watched the figures enter the room and take their seats. Their hiding spot was perfect, giving them a prime view of everything about to take place.

Several well-dressed men and women of different ages sat around the table with Aunty Binta at the head, Olu to her right and Daba to her left. They chatted about things Yomi didn't fully understand until Aunty Binta stood up. "Now, should we start? Naka ngon si."

"Good evening," came the polite chorus back.

"Sorry to bring you here so late. Recent events have given cause to bring the Gambian branch of the Sacred Beast League together," Aunty Binta said.

Inside the cupboard, Yomi and Kayode exchanged a surprised look as Aunty Binta nodded towards Daba, before taking a seat.

"Ninki Nanka has been confirmed as missing."

Yomi looked at the group's varied expressions at Daba's announcement. Their sadness, shock and anger were clear. "There have been several reports that the King has gone silent and the river is being punished for it. Flooding and extreme damage to the environment. And there was a witness to the crime – Olu's niece."

"Obviously, the Beast Hunters' Guild are inv—" Olu announced.

"Olu." A woman Yomi recognized from their visit to the hunters' headquarters interrupted. "They would have taken responsibility if they were involved. Everyone knows they don't seem to value secrecy any more."

"My niece and nephew found a treasure trove of Beast parts in an underground chamber. There was even the skeleton of a Yarcoss taken from protected grounds. If that's not a violation of the pact, I don't know what is!"

"Your niece and nephew, Olu?" someone questioned in a harsh voice.

"Ah..." Olu suddenly went quiet.

"Such a place is not appropriate for children," another member raged.

Olu bristled. "Without them, we would never have found that evidence."

"For their own safety, they must be kept out of our affairs," Aunty Binta ordered.

"The hunters are an issue, Madam Ngom," Daba added, steering the conversation back to Ninki Nanka's disappearance.

"They're spreading their reach further across the continent. We have to act now..." Olu started.

"Not this again." Aunty Binta sounded weary.

"We must take stronger action against the Guild's breaking of the pact," Daba warned.

"Once they get rid of the Sacred Nkara, who else stands in their way?" Olu declared. "The truce is over and Yinza is the only way to fight the Guild."

"Yinza is unpredictable and therefore dangerous and that is why we cannot use it, even against the Guild," Aunty Binta explained.

"If we don't act soon, there'll be no Africa to protect!" Olu stressed.

Aunty Binta silenced him with a gentle hand. "We will deal with the Guild accordingly, and we will work out the differences within the S.B.L. another time. But first we *must* find Ninki Nanka."

The room sat in wary silence – everyone's eyes nervously bouncing back and forth between Madam Binta and Olu.

Eventually Daba piped up. "OK, so. Are we all agreed?"

"Waaw," the others replied.

"S.B.L. will take action quickly. Our priority is bringing harmony back to the river; it's the only way the country can survive." With a nod, Aunty Binta dismissed the group and everyone exited the room.

In the closet's darkness, Yomi took a deep breath, taking it all in, while Kayode was clearly freaked out. "Yomi, we should've never gone down to that chamber."

"You heard them, without us, they wouldn't have found that stuff."

"That doesn't mean we should get more involved!" Kayode replied in a hurried whisper.

"That's *exactly* what it means."

"We could just enjoy the rest of our holiday..."

"This is the first bit of fun we've had. And it's important fun. So will you help me or not?"

Kayode groaned. The beach of his dreams was slipping further and further away. "OK. I'll help you."

"Yes! We can do this, Kay," Yomi said triumphantly. "We're going to find the Dragon King!"

"No, you are not!" Yomi and Kayode froze in terror as the door swung open to a furious Uncle Olu.

There was a painful silence over the breakfast table. Their uncle had said only a few words to them as he drank his coffee. After he had caught them last night, Olu had marched them to their room. He'd said if this happened again, he would send them back to London!

"Kayode, Olorunyomi." Immediately, Yomi

stopped eating her slice of tapalapa bread, while Kayode dropped his half-eaten akara sandwich back on to his plate. "Uncle Daba and I are going back to the Beast Hunters' headquarters. So you'll be staying here with Mrs Sanyang."

"OK, we will be on our best behaviour." Yomi smiled innocently.

Kayode looked at his sister suspiciously until she kicked him underneath the table. "Sorry! Have a good day, Uncle," he said through gritted teeth.

"And another thing before I leave."

"Yes, Uncle," Yomi and Kayode said together.

"Never sneak into our meetings again. I'm serious, this is for your protection. They are not for your ears." With that he stalked out of the room.

After breakfast, the pair moved to the library to do their summer homework under the watchful eyes of Mrs Sanyang who had a low tolerance for silliness. Yet underneath, Yomi sensed a warmth to the housekeeper.

"Fractions! Why do teachers do this to us?" Kayode cried into the large desk.

"Because you have to learn, so get on with it," Mrs Sanyang chided. "When you finish your work for the day, you can have lunch, and then it's your free time. We have bikes out the back if you want to go for a ride."

As soon as Mrs Sanyang left the room, Yomi closed her workbook, marched towards one of the library ladders and started to climb. Once at the top she started pulling out books.

"*History of African Dragon*s. Catch!" She dropped the book towards the ground where Kayode miraculously caught it.

"You could have knocked me out!"

"You're alive, aren't you? *African Waters and Their Secrets*. Heads up!"

She grabbed one of the rails, gave a mighty tug and the ladder swooshed itself to the next column of books. "*The Rise of the Beast Hunter!*"

"How do you even know where the books are?" Kayode asked.

"There's a diagram engraved on the table."

Yomi's hand paused when she saw something metallic poking out of the bookcase in front of her, and she pulled it out to look at it properly. The entire book was metal but it was deceptively light. Its front cover was made up of a collection of patterns with a map of Africa at its centre. The words 'Beast Atlas' were printed on it in a foil lettering. On the side there was an unusual mechanical contraption – a lock like she had never seen before. At the top of the book, there was a luminous green eye staring right up at her, almost daring her to look inside.

"*Beast Atlas* coming down." Yomi dropped it but Kayode wasn't paying attention. The book smashed to the floor with a booming thud.

"Kay!"

"Sorry! I was looking at this: *The Seas of Nyami Nyami.*" He ran to the spot where the atlas landed. "But this is waaay cooler."

"You should have been paying attention," Yomi grumbled as she climbed back down the ladder.

She snatched the book from Kayode. "I couldn't open it."

"Maybe try this?" Kayode pulled out the metal pick from the Beast Hunters' headquarters.

"You kept it?" Yomi said, surprised.

"Of course I did!"

"Still, it'd be pretty convenient if it worked," Yomi muttered.

Kayode slid the pick into the lock and after a few moments of tinkering the book unlocked. He gave a satisfied smile just as a cloud of dust puffed up in their faces. Kayode coughed dramatically.

Once the air cleared, they began to read the first page.

BEAST CLASSIFICATION

The Nkara of our world are many and divided into two categories: Grand and Sacred.

Sacred Beasts are rare and their power is supreme.

Types of Beast:

1. **Ancients:** Creatures whose origins can be traced back centuries and, in many cases, to the beginning of the recorded world. These creatures have outlasted dynasties and empires and usually have secrets and lost knowledge about the world.

2. **Spirits:** Creatures with magical powers which vary from beast to beast i.e. healing, enchantment and illusions. These creatures can also be a disembodied spirit, which possesses objects and animals.

ZIMEKI
(SPIRIT)

**KOUPÉ
(SHAPESHIFTER)**

3. **SHAPESHIFTERS:** Beings with the ability to change their physical form and appearance at will. Shapeshifting can occur via many different methods such as shedding of skin and hair, mimicking or literally turning into the creature in question. It is important to note that shapeshifting can also exist with magical and artificial intervention. In this case there will be use of a talisman or amulet. Yinza plays a role here.

4. **DRAGONS:** Creatures which share characteristics of being large, serpentine, winged (can usually fly), clawed, scaly, horned, have a tail and capable of expelling a substance (i.e. fire and water).

5. **TROLLS:** Creatures which range from dwarfs to giants but usually take humanoid form. Can be highly intelligent and dangerous. Extremely adaptable to various habitats in which man cannot survive for long.

6. **MUTANTS:** Creatures which have similarities to other animals but have been manipulated to embody excessive power via either strength or intelligence.

**TEGGU
(TROLL)**

Yomi turned the page. Here the atlas had been divided into countries. She turned the metallic tinted pages further until she got to The Gambia and found the river. Images of Ninki Nanka flashed across the pages in some sort of holographic dance.

"There's that word Yinza again. What *is* it?" Yomi wondered.

"Probably something creepy... Look, it says this is the part of the river where Ninki Nanka lives." Kayode pointed at the map of the river stretching across the double page of The Gambia.

"Even though he's not there, there might be clues still at the river." Yomi turned away from the atlas to look at a local map and plan their route.

"I don't like hippos," Kayode suddenly said loudly.

"Hippos! Why are you talking about hippos?" Yomi asked.

"Because hippos can swallow you whole and apparently there is a Grand Nkara called Nyanya, a spirit hippo, who lives by the river and knows everything."

"Is that in the atlas?" Yomi turned back to Kayode.

"Yeah, on the next page." He handed her the metal book and Yomi saw how the map of the river continued past the first double spread and on to the next few pages. The river actually seemed to *move* through the pages. It depicted the location of Nyanya's lair, where she gave guidance to the fisher people on the river.

"That's it, Kay. We need to speak to her," Yomi concluded, marking Nyanya's lair on her map with an X.

"You want us to go to the river and speak to a spirit." Kayode looked at her weirdly.

"We can ask her for help. I'm sure she wants Ninki Nanka back too. She's guardian to the fisher people and Ninki Nanka is King of the River – they must need each other." Yomi smiled, excited for their next move. "Let's grab the bikes and go after lunch!"

"No." Kayode shook his head.

"But you love being by the water!"

"Not like that!" Kayode exclaimed.

"What's the worst that can happen?" Yomi queried.

He looked at her in horror, and Yomi could see his imagination going wild with things which could go very wrong. "I really don't like hippos."

CHAPTER 7

RIVERLANDS

Yomi and Kayode cycled past a raft of otters along the riverbank. Mrs Sanyang had told them she expected them back by 6 p.m. for dinner, which only gave them a few hours to find Nyanya.

Pelicans, ibises, herons and storks welcomed the pair to their world, flying over their heads and guiding them down the river's shores until the marshes along the riverbank turned brittle and dry. The river's air didn't taste salty but bitter like expired limes.

Yomi knew that the river was the spine of the country, its waters serving as the lifeblood to all of The Gambia. Whether it be fisher people throwing large nets into the water or the oyster catchers dropping their fishing pots to the bottom of the river, everybody relied on the river. Seeing the river absent of all of this revealed the damage done.

"We need to find a canoe, and quickly," Yomi instructed, but nowhere would allow them to rent one. The locals explained that, given the disappearance of Ninki Nanka, no one was going on to the water.

"The river is more dangerous when he is not here," one fisherman warned them sternly.

Eventually Yomi and Kayode dropped their bikes close to a bunch of mahogany trees, looking worse for wear with their giant brown roots tangling their way through the soil. They edged closer towards the river. Ninki Nanka's absence was causing everything to fall apart. The birds had departed, leaving behind deformed-looking bullfrogs and lizards skittering around, while vultures circled hungrily high above.

"Why does that frog have three eyes?" Kayode asked as it blinked at him.

Yomi didn't have an answer, because just at that moment she spotted a lone linta with *two* hooded heads skating over the river, before taking off up into the sky. They usually travelled in groups. Seeing one by itself suggested the others had left, panicked at their protector's absence.

"This is getting freaky, Yomi," Kayode said, his tone on edge.

"We *will* find a canoe," Yomi said, determined to find one no matter what. They searched through the marshes and creeks until *finally* they found a small, abandoned canoe. Together, Yomi and Kayode pushed the boat to the edge of the river.

"Young ones should be careful so close to the water."

The siblings nearly jumped out of their skin. Hesitantly they turned around to find an elderly man with shiny brown skin and cloudy eyes.

"Are you talking to us?" Kayode asked warily.

"Yes," the man responded

"We'll be careful. Thank you."

Yomi's nerves were beginning to get the better of her. What had she got them into? The atmosphere on the river was unnerving. The unfamiliarity of the creatures around them, the barren, decaying nature of the riverbank. And then this man who had appeared from nowhere.

"We need to hurry if we are going to get to the hippo," Kayode said.

"How do you know about Nyanya?" the stranger interrupted.

"We read it in—" Yomi elbowed Kayode to be quiet.

"You are right. You mustn't go telling strangers your secrets." The old man's eyes intensified and for a moment Yomi thought they turned gold.

"I am sure you know Ninki Nanka is missing," Yomi declared.

"Yes. The river will die if the King is not found," the old man warned. "So many have fallen to *their* hands. If humans are not careful, perhaps the world will enter a new era. One without humanity."

"But it's not all humans. It's just Beast Hunters," Kayode said deliberately.

"We're on the Nkara's side and that's why we need

92

Nyanya's help to find Ninki Nanka," Yomi pressed.

"Indeed. Perhaps you *can* match the willpower of those who took the Dragon King. I wish you good luck on the way to Nyanya, but be careful. The river is full of danger."

The canoe sailed over the now silent but murky waters. The further Yomi and Kayode drifted downstream, the more plant life surrounded them. This part of the waterway seemed unnervingly bountiful and the air was heavy with an ominous silence.

As they went along, they spotted a group of crocodiles watching them hungrily from the riverbank.

"Kayode. *Do. Not. Stop. Paddling*," Yomi urged through gritted teeth.

But just as Kayode was about to get going again the predators started slinking into the water.

"Yomi!" Kayode squeaked.

Yomi's heart hammered in her chest as the crocodiles headed straight for them.

What *were* they going to do?

As Yomi looked around, trying to find an escape route, her attention was abruptly interrupted by a kind of buuuurble. Big bubbles floated up, popping on the water's surface until...

Everything went still.

Suddenly, there was a violent swirl of water. The reptiles were dragged down, each crocodile whipping round uncontrollably as they tried to thrash free of whatever was sucking them beneath.

"Oh-my-gosh-oh-my-gosh-oh-my-gosh, Yomi, what is going on?" Kayode screamed.

"I don't know!" And at that point she felt something large bump underneath the boat.

She and Kayode held their breath.
The crocodiles had gone but now several
long pincer-like arms were reaching out of the water,
wrapping themselves around the craft with a vice-
like grip!

As Yomi and Kayode clung to each other, the oversized, bodyless claws twisted and shook the small vessel violently, throwing them about until Yomi, with nothing to hold on to, was tossed straight into the water.

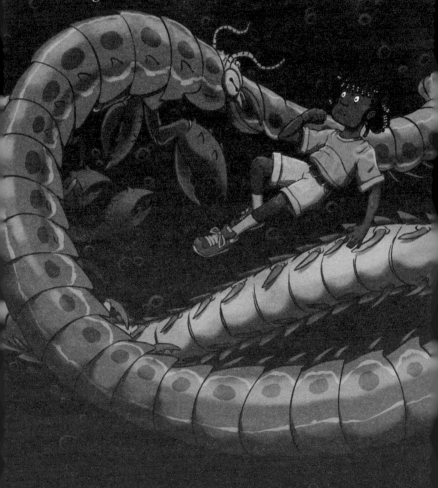

"Yomi!" Kayode's cry was the last thing she heard before slipping into the river's depths.

Within the darkness of the waters, Yomi tried not to panic. She knew that if she did, she'd very quickly run out of breath. She looked around, trying to get her bearings, until she spotted two lights directly below her. As she stared at the glowing bulbs, to her horror they turned into two blood-red eyes staring right at her. There was a moment of stillness and with a dull sounding whooOOOOOOsh an elongated mandible struck out to snatch her!

Yomi gave an underwater scream, wildly flailing her arms and legs in an attempt to stop herself being captured. It reached out with a claw again but Yomi dodged it and poked its right eye in response.

Out of nowhere, Yomi felt something brush against her face. She looked up and saw the fibres of a net. Without a moment's hesitation she grabbed on to it and with a strong tug she was dragged back up to the surface, barely escaping the pincers snapping at her feet.

Yomi took a deep intake of air. "Oh, Kay, thank you. So *so* much." She wheezed.

"Are you all right?" Kayode asked.

"Smart move." Yomi nodded and coughed while her brother slapped her back.

"Arabella Carter, volume seventeen, when she saves her friend from killer squids in Norway," he explained.

Yomi turned to smile at her brother, but very quickly her gratitude turned to alarm.

The clawed creature was not finished! It raised its enormous pincers once again and this time a watery growl vibrated around them.

"GRRRRRRRRRRRRR."

"Paddle, Kay," Yomi rasped at her brother. "Paddle for your life!"

Yomi banged her oar on one of the claws with as much force as she could, momentarily causing the creature to release its grip.

Yomi and Kayode didn't hesitate but their sheer terror messed with their paddle strokes, causing them to row out of sync.

"One, *two*, three, one, *two*, three," Yomi chanted giving them a rhythm to follow and miraculously they found themselves across the swamp. As quickly as they could they jumped out of the canoe, pulling themselves up the riverbank on to safe and solid ground.

Breathing heavily, Yomi looked back at the boat, amazed it was still in one piece. She was dripping wet but gave herself a once-over and then made sure her brother was also uninjured.

"I nearly lost you!"

Kayode said angrily, grabbing then gripping her in a tight hug. "What would I do without you?"

Yomi could hear the sob in his voice. Her brother never got angry, and seeing him like this was something she never wanted to do again.

"You'd not get into danger any more, that's for sure," Yomi tried to joke but it failed. Finally she hugged him back. "I'm not going anywhere. Especially if you are with me. It's going to be all right."

"I hope so." Kayode held on a little longer before eventually sitting back and wiping his eyes. "So what do we do now?" he asked.

"What we came here for. Let's find Nyanya," Yomi declared.

CHAPTER 8
NYANYA

"Do you think we're in the right place?" Kayode peered over Yomi's shoulder to look at the map. While Yomi had dried quickly under the summer sun, the map was still soaking. They could just make out they were near the X Yomi had marked for Nyanya's lair. The mud on the riverbank was softer too. Perfect for hippos.

"I don't know but I hope so!" Yomi's nerves continued to bubble away in her stomach, their narrow escape from the unknown clawed Beast keeping her on edge.

"Do you think this is even safe?" Kayode asked.

"It's better than back there," Yomi replied.

"Yomi, a giant claw attached to who knows what

tried to snatch us. There's a reason no one can find Nyanya's lair. We also don't know what this hippo is capable of!"

Kayode was right but there wasn't much Yomi could do about it now.

They reached a tidal flat with a cave close by. Thickets of bamboo and other reeds grew around it, but several sections were either bent or squashed like they had gone up against a massive weight and lost.

"This has to be it," Yomi said as they headed towards the lair. Not far from the entrance, a stunning reddish-gold bird was perched on a broken branch. It had a gold ribbon-like tail of feathers which touched the ground but as Yomi's eyes followed it down, she noticed something unusual.

"Its feet, Kay. It doesn't have talons," Yomi whispered nervously.

"Wait, are those lion's claws?" Kayode asked hesitantly.

"I think it's a Kiross," Yomi whispered, thinking of the legendary Grand Nkara from their grandma's stories.

With its long wingspan outstretched, the bird made a screeching sound as if celebrating some sort of victory. Yomi examined the fiery gold feathers with black streaks covering its entire body, taking in its large claws and its piercing gold eyes. The bird held her gaze.

Yomi could tell Kayode was petrified. So was she!

"OK. Let's stop staring and just walk calmly straight ahead." She tried to sound as reassuring as possible.

"If Nyanya makes a go for us, run in a zigzag," Kayode said.

"I don't know if that's the right animal. I think you just have to hide from hippos," Yomi said.

"How are we supposed to hide? We're in *her* lair!"

"Are you sure you want to go in there?"

Yomi and Kayode both yelped. The question had come from the Kiross.

"You can talk?" Kayode squeaked.

"I'm speaking to you right now, aren't I?"

"Who are you?" Yomi questioned.

The Nkara leaned forwards as if to answer. "Come inside and all will be revealed." It flew off its perch and into the cave. Yomi quickly followed, dragging Kayode with her.

"Mistress Nyanya, am nanu visitors kan am dikka pur dimbal," the Kiross announced the pair as they entered the cave.

"I only help fisher people and these children are no fisher people," roared a voice from the darkness. The voice was huge and as it echoed around the dark space, Yomi swore she could hear the scurrying of little creatures running away in fear. She could sense Kayode holding his breath.

"We need your help to find Ninki Nanka," Yomi declared.

"*You* do not demand anything from *me*. Take your commands elsewhere," Nyanya proclaimed.

"Do you not care about Ninki Nanka?" Yomi argued.

"Are you challenging me?" Nyanya's voice turned cold.

"No. No, No. Of course not," Kayode stuttered as he stepped back, dragging his sister's arm with him.

"Leave now before I *crush* you." Nyanya took a step out of the shadows. Though they couldn't quite see her, they saw her outline. Large didn't quite cut it.

"We're not leaving," Yomi piped up. She had

to stand her ground.

"Why do you wish to help Ninki Nanka? What do you humans get out of it?" Nyanya probed.

Yomi looked at Kayode, whose nervous expression changed into a supportive smile, and took a deep breath before she began. "My family are storytellers, we've always been told the great stories of this continent. Ninki Nanka is one of those stories. His life is important to all life here. All Nkara need to be protected because..."

"Because what?" Nyanya sneered.

"Well, because at the end of the day, we all have to share and take care of this world."

Nyanya gave a hearty laugh and stepped out of the dark.

Yomi and Kayode gasped. Before them, Nyanya's belly loomed round like the sun; the hide covering her flesh glowed like burnt gold. Stumpy legs supported her gigantic body. She was indeed a very grand beast.

"So." Nyanya chuckled. "You are brave. And you certainly have honour. Don't they, Mustafa?"

Nyanya looked at her avian attendant, who flew away from the hippo and landed in front of the pair in a flash of yellow light. In a blink of an eye the Kiross was the old man from the riverbank.

"You're a shapeshifter!" Yomi declared.

"Mezamorphi to be exact." Mustafa turned to the golden hippo. "Mistress Nyanya, I believe these children are true protectors of Nkara. They survived the Gulegese on the river."

Nyanya looked impressed.

"Do you know what happened to Ninki Nanka?" Yomi asked.

"I think Ninki Nanka has been imprisoned."

"But where?"

"I suspect he's in the Skyfort. The castle in the sky."

"But why aren't the Sacred Beast League looking there?" Yomi asked.

"Most believe the Nkara still control it, which is far from the truth. It has very recently fallen into the hands of the Beast Hunters' Guild. And only hunters would dare launch an attack on a Sacred Nkara like Ninki Nanka."

"So Uncle Olu was right!" said Yomi.

"Ninki Nanka was bound by moonlight and trapped with the shackles of darkness," Nyanya continued.

"I saw it! The night he was taken," Yomi exclaimed.

"The Guild have wanted Ninki Nanka for a long time. You know the history?"

The two of them nodded.

"If you wish to climb into the skies, you will need sky rope of your own, but you will have to go further upriver for this." Nyanya approached the pair, her body bulky and huge. "To find sky rope, there is only one place in all of The Gambia it can be obtained."

Yomi and Kayode waited eagerly for the location.

"Mansa's Stone."

"The monument built during the Mali Empire?" Yomi asked in awe.

"Yes, Mustafa will guide you there." The attendant bowed to the hippo and gestured for the pair to leave the cave as Nyanya turned and shuffled back into the darkness, bringing their audience to an abrupt end.

"Wait!" Yomi had a sudden thought. "Do you think it could have been the Beast Prime who took Ninki Nanka?"

"He now controls the Skyfort so I'd imagine that to be the case. Do you not think it was?"

"I don't know," Yomi said quietly.

Nyanya paused and turned her mighty head towards them. "You'll soon find out."

"Boy, if you don't stop talking, I'll feed you to the Gulegese myself," Mustafa muttered irritably as Kayode asked *another* question. "Now look, we are *here*."

Yomi and Kayode looked before them. Situated slightly below them on a low hill lay Mansa's Stone!

The fortress-like structure was immense. Surrounded by an almost impenetrable swell of fragrant leaves from the acacia and kapok trees, the foliage came together to form an extra natural barrier to the stone's enemies. The building was a series of minaret towers, seemingly sky-high, slender columns built from solid blocks of mud brick.

Mustafa turned his regal head of feathers towards the pair and gave them careful instructions on how to reach the Stone by foot. "Remember, there are lots of outposts like this all over Africa hidden in plain sight."

"Thank you," Yomi and Kayode said together.

"I wish you good fortune, young Beast protectors," Mustafa said before he swept up into the air. Yomi and Kayode both watched until he was out of sight.

"We don't have much time until dinner," Kayode reminded Yomi.

"Then let's do this," she replied.

Following Mustafa's directions, the pair headed into the bush, cutting through the mini savannah of trees, up the hill and then around the back to the smallest of the towers.

They stepped inside the Stone's inner walls, where gold dust peppered the air. Elaborate pieces of bronze and wooden furniture were stationed around the giant ground-floor room. Light shone through several of the Stone's windows on to this almost hidden part of the city.

Behind the single counter sat the only other person in the room, who happened to be reading the latest issue of Arabella Carter.

"Can I help you?" The man lowered his comic to reveal he was wearing a dark

gold visor. He wore a bright printed jacket with a long golden chain cutting across his body from his shoulder to way below his right arm.

"Um, please can I have some sky rope?" Yomi asked.

"Sure, how much?" the man turned the page of the comic.

"Well, er, enough to get to the sky."

The man put down his comic and looked in their direction, as if only just registering what they had asked for. "What would two little kids like you need to be going up into the *sky* for?"

"Exploring," Yomi answered quickly.

"Huh." The man pulled out a silver safe the size of a small suitcase from behind the counter. "Exploring? The only business going on up there now is Beast business."

He carried on staring at them, while pretty impressively typing in a long passcode. Then the case popped open and he pulled out the snake-like rope. It shone with the brightness of the moon.

"Wow! How big is it in there?" Kayode exclaimed, trying to peer into the suitcase.

"Huge," the man answered.

"Thank you." Yomi put her hands out to take it, but the man immediately threw the rope back in the box and slammed it shut.

"You do not get something for nothing. Buy, sell or *fair trade*." He went back to reading his comic.

"But we don't have anything," Yomi complained.

Surely they couldn't have come this far only to be told they had to go home.

"Do you have any of the golden volumes?" Kayode asked.

The man dropped his comic. "Don't joke around."

Yomi looked at her younger brother, confused. What was he talking about?

Kayode wasn't joking around. He dug his hand into his pocket and pulled out a notebook-sized comic. "Arabella Carter, golden volume six."

"The one when she breaks out of the jail in Laos?" Even with the visor on, they could tell the man's eyes were popping out of their sockets!

"Yep," Kayode answered.

Yomi knew that volume was a rarity. She was touched her brother was prepared to give it away to help them on their mission.

"Now you kids are talking my language. Take all the sky rope you want!" He put his hand out to take the comic but Kayode pulled it away at the last second. "Hold up. *You* said a *fair* trade."

Kayode mimicked the trader's words with a smile.

The man's shoulders hunched in frustration. "OK, fine. Let's trade for it." He opened up the suitcase again and handed Yomi a device covered in dark grey material. Yomi switched it on and the black-and-white screen lit up with the three dials underneath it spinning erratically.

"That's a Beast scanner. It's used to scan for Nkara at high altitudes. You're going to need it if the stories of the Skyfort are true!"

"Thank you so much!" Yomi said.

"Can I have the comic now? Then I'll cut some sky rope for you."

Kayode handed over the comic and the man went off to finish the deal.

Yomi's mind was spinning at the size of the overwhelming task ahead of them. They had to climb a rope to a castle in the *sky*!

"Kay, do you think we can do this?"

Kayode chuckled in disbelief until he realized she was serious. "Of course we can."

"Look at all the trouble we've got into." Doubt was creeping in, especially after Kay had given away something he loved so much.

"Don't you mean all the amazing stuff we've seen and *done*? All because of you!" Kayode urged. "We – *you* – can definitely do this!"

Yomi smiled at her brother, knowing how lucky she was to have him.

"But do you have any idea *how* we are going to do this?" Kayode asked.

"Well, first of all we go to the Skyfort," said Yomi. "We find the Beast Prime – I'm thinking let's say we want to be his apprentices. Then we can look around, find Ninki Nanka and free him."

"Not a bad plan in theory..." Kayode replied.

Their moment was interrupted when the man returned to hand over their purchase. Yomi took the moon-coloured rope, noticing it felt hot in her hands.

"Come back any time if you want to do more business. Make sure you bring more of these!" the man said, holding up his new treasure and grinning.

"Thank you!" Yomi packed the rope and Beast scanner into her rucksack.

"Oh, and let me give my newest and favourite customers a word of warning. The sky rope works only once. Once climbed, *poof!* It will disappear. To use it just throw it out of the highest room of your home and it will extend up to the heavens."

"You're sure?" Kayode looked uneasy.

The rope couldn't have been any longer than ten metres, but the man assured them it would reach their destination.

"It will work, trust me. Instruments of the moon have been crafted by the most skilled Yinza users to have ever lived. These instruments never fail in their intended task. Everything else? That depends on the user."

CHAPTER 9

SKYFORT

When Olu entered Yomi and Kayode's bedroom, they could tell he was surprised to see them already tucked up in their beds.

"Do anything interesting today?" their uncle asked.

"Nothing really, just looked around town," Yomi said vaguely.

They had made it back just before six. And with Olu gone and Mrs Sanyang busy, they'd even had time to roam the house looking for additional tools for their rescue mission.

"I'm sorry, guys, this has been a pretty lame holiday for you."

"It's been interesting." Kayode yawned.

"You sure about that, Kay?" Olu laughed, but Yomi

noticed he still looked sad.

"How's the search for Ninki Nanka going?" she asked.

"Not good at all," their uncle confessed, and he came to sit down next to them on Yomi's bed.

"I'm sorry," she said.

"What are you saying sorry for?"

"Sneaking around, I guess?" Yomi offered. She felt guilty for still secretly investigating Ninki Nanka – especially when their uncle had expressly told them not to. She wanted to tell him everything but how would he react? Would he send them back to London?

Olu smiled. "Yeah, we never talked about that properly, did we? I should have never even taken you to the Guild's headquarters. I opened you up to a world you shouldn't know about. Especially not now. How could I expect you not to go explore? Your dad and I used to sneak around all the time when we were kids, so I can't be too hard on you both. But I meant what I said. Do not get involved. Let the adults, the *professionals*, deal with this situation."

"Hold on. Sneak around with Dad?" Yomi questioned.

Olu looked nervous. "You should ask him next time you see him."

"But we could help you." Yomi couldn't help but be irritated. She knew they were closer to the answer than the S.B.L. and that maybe their information could help their uncle persuade Aunty Binta the hunters were involved.

"This is dangerous stuff, it's beyond you. Please leave it to us," Olu explained. "I wanted to show you adventure but I went too far. I mean, if your parents knew..." He gave a low whistle. "You must forget everything you have seen. Forget about the Beast Hunters. Forget about the Sacred Beast League. Just forget *all* of this exists!"

Yomi crossed her arms underneath the covers. That their uncle didn't want to share anything with them hurt rather than annoyed her. Yomi knew she was making the right choice – she was going to prove that *nothing* was beyond them.

"Fine." Yomi looked to Kayode, who also gave a single nod of his head.

"Thank you. I appreciate it. Now off to sleep." Olu stood up quickly. "I have some more work to do." He moved towards the door but stopped. "I love you both very much."

"Love you too," they responded as he left the room.

After a moment of stillness, Yomi pulled a torch from beneath her pillow and shone it at Kayode. "Ready?"

"I guess," he said with a nervous thumbs up.

Throwing off their covers, they were both dressed for a rescue. From underneath their beds they grabbed rucksacks filled with supplies found around the house, including two-way radios, a first-aid kit, torches, night and magnifying goggles and compasses. During their search of the house, they had also found a box taken from the Beast Hunters' Guild. Inside were two pairs of leather gloves with solid steel claws sticking out of the knuckles and thick bronze-coloured circles on the fingers and thumbs, which stuck to Yomi's hand when she touched it. She looked at their haul, impressed by everything they had gathered. Gadgets *and* information.

"Are *you* ready?" Kayode asked Yomi this time.

"I was born ready," Yomi replied with a grin and turned towards their skyward exit. She opened their window to the darkness.

Kayode handed over the sky rope and, after counting to three, Yomi launched it with all her might. Up and up it went, until...

Thwomp.

It dropped back down and hit the ground.

"That's not supposed to happen!" Kayode shout-whispered.

Yomi was about to pull it back up to try again when the rope began to unfurl upwards, rising into the sky.

"It's working." Yomi's eyes brightened as she followed the rope rising like a balloon above their heads. "It's *working*!"

Yomi tied the other end of the rope to her bedpost in a series of tight knots to make sure it was secure.

"Here we go. Don't. Look. Down," Yomi told Kayode.

Slowly they climbed, trying not to fall. It was a long way to the ground! Yomi started to think that this was a lot easier than expected.

Until the rope began to shudder and shake.

Yomi could feel the vibrations of the rope moving through her hands and legs.

Abruptly, the rope buckled, flattening out so it was as though they were riding a wild stallion. For just a moment they were still and then ...

... they were OFF!
Dropping down and
picking back up several times,
the rope moved at lightning speed with
a mind of its own. It never stayed still!
Loop-the-loops followed by slaloms kept
them going at a pace until eventually the
vibrations slowed to a stop. With a jolt,
the rope begun sloping upwards,
projecting them higher into the sky.

"Can you believe this? It's like a ride,"
Yomi called out in wonder.

"No, it's waaay better!" Kayode shouted
above the wind.

With a tremendous boost they shot further
up into the clouds. Yomi stretched one arm wide
as they flew past the bright moon lighting up the
sky around them. They were on top of the world.

"Woohoooooooooo!!!" Yomi screamed into the
night. "This is *the* best adventure EVEEEEEER!"

Soon an outline came into view on the horizon. There it was: the Skyfort. Surrounded by swirling clouds, the puffs of white acted like a protective wall. The moonlight bounced off the fort's solid exterior of gold and steel, which sat on a foundation of granite-like stone and a giant black cog. The imposing structure filled the sky, almost impossibly dominating its surroundings. It was intimidating!

"Look at it, Kayode!" The Skyfort's walls glowed against the night sky, with its towers rising higher than anything Yomi had ever seen on Earth.

The rope slowed its trajectory and came to deposit them in the castle yard, an open plain of clouds. Yomi tentatively touched them. They were fluffy and soft but heavy. As soon as she squeezed, however, they split into a thousand minature puffs. How were they not sinking through? She looked over at Kayode. Typically he was throwing himself around, bouncing on the cloud floor like it was a trampoline.

"Hurry, Kay, we might not have much time!"

As they reached the Skyfort's entrance, a giant iron door awaited them. Before Yomi could stop him, Kayode rushed forwards and banged on it.

"Wai— What did you do that for?" But they had no time to argue. The doors had swung open.

"*Hadim?*"

Despite his age, the boy stood with the poise of a warrior, dressed in a yellow battle-ready tunic.

"What are you doing here?" Hadim asked suspiciously. Clearly he wasn't happy with his uninvited guests.

Yomi had to think quickly – this wasn't part of her plan! She took a deep breath before speaking. "We're here to see your dad."

"My dad?" Hadim looked confused. "He isn't here."

"Well, er, where is he?"

"I don't know."

"How do you not know where your dad is?" Kayode asked.

"That's just how it is." Did Yomi detect a hint of sadness?

"When is he back?" Yomi probed.

"Hold up, who *are* you – Arabella Carter? What's with all these questions?"

"Nyanya said—" Yomi began.

"Wait! Nyanya, the spirit hippo? You'd better come in!" Hadim waved them inside with a false smile. "Don't touch anything, though."

Only a fool would have tried to touch anything anyway. It was like the walls were alive.

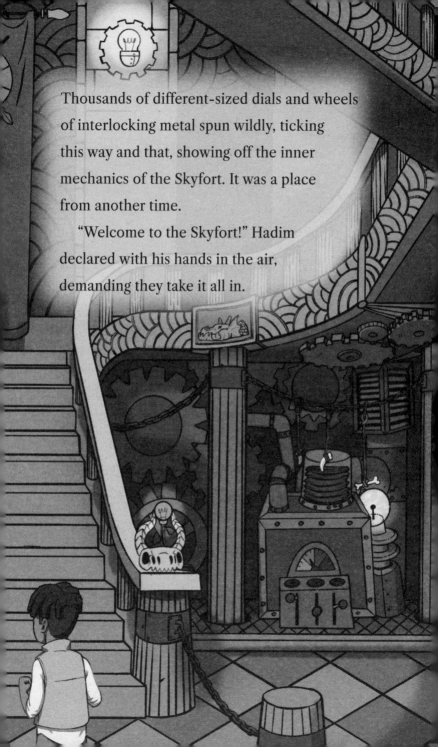

Thousands of different-sized dials and wheels of interlocking metal spun wildly, ticking this way and that, showing off the inner mechanics of the Skyfort. It was a place from another time.

"Welcome to the Skyfort!" Hadim declared with his hands in the air, demanding they take it all in.

"When was this place made?" Kayode asked in awe as they followed Hadim inside.

"My dad built it when he was elected Beast Prime," Hadim explained. The noise of intricate unlocking and grating metal sounded in the background. For the life of her, Yomi couldn't quite understand how all this had been set in motion. It seemed like nothing here was from the present, let alone this dimension.

"The Skyfort is powered by iron panels on top of the fort, which capture the rays of the moon and sun."

"But how is it floating? How did he build it?" Kayode questioned. Yomi wondered if Hadim would be honest and admit that Nkara had built it.

"Um, well, *OK*. If you must know, it was kind of here already. He just had to take it from a brigade of Crix trolls and then make some, well, improvements," Hadim confessed.

"Crix trolls?" Yomi looked at Kayode.

"Yeah. You know – the flesh-eating trolls?"

Yomi and Kayode shook their heads.

"Like this!" Hadim suddenly opened another

door off the hallway and pushed them in.

Immediately Yomi and Kayode slapped their palms over their ears as the sound of horrific shrieks greeted them.

Rows of huge brass cages filled with hairy creatures confronted them. Standing at what seemed like twelve feet tall, each Beast possessed four elongated arms.

Their enlarged limbs and sharp nails swung out desperately to get a piece of the duo standing in front of them.

"AAAAARRGGGHHH!!!" Kayode and Yomi screamed.

Suddenly they were back in the hallway and the door had slammed shut.

"Ha! You should have seen your faces." Hadim chuckled. "My dad took down the leader and then decided to keep the rest as pets."

"What kind of deranged pers—" Kayode started but Yomi nudged him quiet and urged him along, keen to keep up with Hadim. This whole place was just plain creepy!

Hadim guided them into a room. "As you can see we're very well stocked: ngulus, rungus, sjamboks, assegais. You name it, we've got it."

Yomi looked at the walls in shock – rifles, clubs, curved swords and whips were displayed like decorations.

Hadim walked further into the room and came to a stop by a lone lever. Heaving it forwards, a metallic series of thunks and churns sounded around them. Slowly, a black, gold and ivory throne rose from the ground, and in front of that, two smaller seats grew so that Yomi and Kayode could also sit.

"So what do you think of the Skyfort?" Hadim asked eagerly.

Yomi ignored the seat and his question. Her plan was falling apart. The Skyfort felt eerie – a Nkara paradise in the sky, it was now a prison for the Nkara it once homed. It was all wrong and they had to get out of here fast. She got to the point. "Where's Ninki Nanka?"

"What— *Why?*" Hadim narrowed his eyes.

"He's here, isn't he? And if he's here – that means

one of the hunters broke the Biji Pact."

At first it seemed like Hadim was about to protest. But instead, he just sneered.

"Wait." Yomi realized they had been wrong. "It was you. *You* kidnapped Ninki Nanka?"

"Hunters don't speak their secrets," he said. "Come with me. I want to show you something." The young hunter led them deeper into the Skyfort, out of the throne room and past large, dominating doors that were camouflaged against the dark walls.

"You still don't get it, why we hunt," he announced.

"It doesn't matter why, killing Nkara is wrong," Yomi protested.

"No! It's the only right thing to do," Hadim countered.

He stopped along a wall and twisted one of the gold cogs. A door appeared and opened. "My dad's trophy room," Hadim said proudly, nodding for them to take a peek.

Yomi had thought the weapons were bad. This time, the walls were decorated with row upon row of different-sized skulls on plinths.

But worse were the stuffed heads
of Nkara mounted celebratorily
on the walls.

Yomi felt sick.

"Ever since I was little, my dad would take me and my sister on hunts. And I knew then that I would become a Beast Hunter like him. Like her. We can take the Nkara's power, and we can rule the world. Humans are supposed to be the dominant species after all."

"They're mad, Yomi!" Kayode whispered.

"You guys have to understand." Hadim picked up a huge skull and Yomi couldn't believe his strength. "Ninki Nanka is one of the most powerful Sacred Nkara. By catching him I can prove to my dad that I can hunt just as well as my sister. I don't care about the Sacred Beast League's stupid pact," he explained.

Yomi realized that no one else knew what Hadim had done. "Can I see Ninki Nanka?"

"Not until my dad does. Anyway, at the moment he's not my problem." Hadim's facial expression changed. "You are..."

Yomi watched the young hunter turn two knobs and point upwards. As she and Kayode cautiously tilted back their heads, a steel cage came crashing towards them.

"Move, Kay!" Yomi launched into her brother, avoiding capture just in time.

"Run while you can, because you will never make it out of the Skyfort," Hadim declared with a maniacal cackle.

Yomi and Kayode dashed out of the trophy room, with only Hadim's laugh chasing after them. Time was running out and it seemed as if the Skyfort had turned against them. As they ran, scythe-like swinging pendulums came out of the walls and iron spikes shot up out of the floor. Hot gushing steam pumped its ways through the corridors, blocking their vision.

Dodging left, then right, jumping, ducking and diving, Yomi and Kayode *just* managed to evade the fort's deadly traps.

"C'mon, we've got to find Ninki Nanka and get out of here!" Yomi yelled.

Spotting a staircase, she grabbed Kayode's hand and headed straight for it. She took the first step down but from the dark below came a roar that chilled her to the bone. Yomi recognized that hellish sound from the night she saw the Dragon King fighting an unknown enemy. Now they were trapped inside that enemy's castle.

CHAPTER 10

TRAPPED

Yomi and Kayode battled their way down the stairs against gales of wind conjured by the castle, hands held up to their faces for protection. Ghostly screams of pain and sadness swirled around them. This was petrifying!

Down and down they went, the spiral stairwell twisting and turning into a never-ending inkiness. Both Yomi and Kayode fumbled for their torches and switched them on.

"I don't like this. I don't like this one bit," Kayode muttered.

As they stumbled and tripped forwards, they soon found themselves in a slightly lighter passageway. It wasn't any less threatening, though. On either side of the corridor there were rows of looming metal doors accompanied by an ominous repetitive ticking sound.

"What's that noise?" Kayode asked Yomi.

"A clock? Grab the scanner, it's time to play with our gadgets."

Kayode quickly dug around in his rucksack and pulled out the Beast scanner. Holding it in the air, he tried to see if he could find Ninki Nanka.

"Come *on*, Kay – don't we just follow a dot or something?"

"It's not that simple! Look, this way, I think..." Kayode started to move forwards when a door sliced shut behind them, sealing them off from the stairs.

"Where did that come from?" The pair looked at each other just as a loud siren went off.

"Run!" Yomi cried over the awful sound and they sprinted down the corridor. Suddenly the walls and doors started to shift and move around like a game of tiles. Even the floor underneath them started to rotate and now, somehow, they seemed to be running along the walls!

"Where's Ninki Nanka?" Yomi panted as they ran.

I'm not sure, it's saying he's moving." Kayode
passed the scanner over.

"It's because the rooms are moving." Yomi
spun round, trying to figure out which way to go.
Suddenly the floor tiles folded out into a labyrinth
of steps, ascending and descending, criss-crossing
and connecting. Yomi and Kayode followed the
steps with
the doors
still shifting
around them.

"This is insane, I can't follow it." Yomi held the scanner up, trying to work out which door the dragon's signal was coming from.

Kayode looked over Yomi's shoulder to see the screen. "It's that one," he shouted, racing for a door far off on the right-hand side.

"Wait, WAIT, Kayode!" Yomi shouted. He'd already run ahead but the door reversed on itself. Yomi collided into Kayode's back as the pair watched the door complete a tricky twist around several other entryways before blending in among the others.

They concentrated hard, keeping their eyes laser-focused on tracking the door that separated them from Ninki Nanka.

"No, he's in there." Yomi pointed at another door shifting right above their heads. She led them back up the rising steps to get closer to it.

"We have to wait for it to drop down, then jump on it."

"What if it moves up instead?"

"Let's just hope it doesn't." As they held their

breath, the screech of gears sent everything around them moving in opposite directions. For once, however, a bit of luck was on their side.

"Jump!" Yomi yelled and they made the leap, reaching out to grab hold of the iron bars at the top of the door.

"AAAAARGH!" Yomi had missed! She was now clinging on to Kayode's waist for dear life. Her heart thumped out of control as the pair hung from the door frame, the floors whizzing around them.

"Yomi, we can't stay like this!" Kayode called out.

"Hold on, Kay, it has to stop at some point." And it did. But the door was now on the ceiling, leaving Kayode hanging in mid-air with Yomi still clinging to his waist.

"Let me just—" Yomi carefully shimmied herself back up Kayode's climbing-frame body to grab on to one of the door frame's iron ornaments which poked outwards.

"Ow! Be careful."

"Oh, shush!" Yomi pressed her ear against the door, through which she could hear another ticking sound. She tried to open the door but it wouldn't budge. "It's not opening."

"Try the lock pick?" Kayode suggested. "It's in my right pocket."

"It won't work *again*," Yomi said.

"Just try!"

Yomi plunged her hand into his pocket and chuckled.

"What could be funny right now?" Kayode cried.

"Your pockets are disgusting. What else is in there?" Yomi said.

Yomi looked through the keyhole but she could see only shadows. She inserted the pick and started jiggling it around until she heard it unlock with a loud click, which echoed through the corridors.

"We're in." Holding on to the door frame, Yomi kicked the door open, allowing them to climb up through the doorway into the room.

Yomi helped Kayode up and the pair dusted themselves off before peering into the gloom.

"Hello?" Yomi called out. Moonlight crept into the room from the window at the top of the wall.

Apart from the ticking, there was silence.

Until... A purr-like grumble came from a corner of the prison.

"Who are you?" a heavy voice slowly curled back.

Yomi took a deep breath, trying to revive her disappearing confidence. Now that the Beast was in front of them, her nerves had almost deserted her. She hadn't seen anything yet!

Gathering herself, she took a small brave step towards the booming voice. "My name is Yomi and this is my brother Kayode, we..." She gulped. "We have come to save you?"

"Please don't eat us." Kayode shivered behind her.

They took another step forwards and there in the light of the moon was the Dragon King in the flesh. They stared in awe.

Ninki Nanka's long body with its scaly skin glowed with a dark blue-green hue. His wings were bent at strange angles due to the confines of his cell. The tall, thick metal bars of the locked giant cage kept the dragon well and truly trapped.

"I do not eat humans," Ninki Nanka replied, showing off his rows of sharp teeth. "You really don't taste good."

Yomi stepped slowly towards the cage, scared but prepared for this moment. As she looked steadily at Ninki Nanka, she gently put a hand through the bars to touch the scratches across his scales.

"We will get you out of here, I promise," she said quietly.

Ninki Nanka watched them with his green eyes. "If you free me, I will reward your assistance."

Yomi didn't doubt him.

Kayode examined the giant bars and the lock at the front of the cage.

"I have something that can help with this." He pulled out the lock pick and got to work to free the dragon. He tinkered for a few minutes before he turned to Yomi.

"It's not working." He tried again, turning the pick both clockwise and anti-clockwise.

"They crafted the lock using Yinza. Your tools won't work here," Ninki Nanka told them. "Yinza magic comes from the moon, the greatest power this world will ever see."

The dragon's words reminded Yomi of what Hadim had said at the party about a force that could change or destroy the world.

Yomi circled the cage, taking in its solid mechanics. She put on one of the Beast Hunter metal gloves, not knowing what else they would have to face. She wanted to be ready to protect Kayode and herself. She followed the trail of golden cogs around the cage, which moved upwards into the wall behind it. All of it – the cage, the walls, the floors, the Skyfort itself – worked together like one big clock. So that was where the ticking came from.

To open the cage, Yomi needed to destroy the mechanism holding it together by creating a gap in its intricate system. But how and with what?

"How did Hadim catch you?" Kayode asked, curious as to how such a powerful Beast could have been captured.

"That boy is a demon," Ninki Nanka revealed. "We battled in the air; it was a mighty fight but he had access to an instrument of the moon."

"Sky rope?" Kayode asked.

"Yes, he activated a machine from the Skyfort, which let out miles of it into the night where it pursued me across the sky. When the rope touched me, I was left powerless and with no strength at all." They could hear his rage burning through his words.

Suddenly there was a huge clang as the door to their prison flung open. A spear gushed through the air, missing Kayode's ear by a millimetre and embedded itself in the ground right by Ninki Nanka's tail.

Hadim smiled. "In the Beast Hunters' Guild, we show our enemies no mercy."

CHAPTER 11
THE RESCUE

"You can't keep a Beast locked up!" Kayode shouted.

"And who will free him?" Hadim dangled the keys in his hands, before removing a spear attached to his back. "Are you going to challenge me to battle? Because I will crush you like an ant." Hadim pointed the spear at Kayode.

"A battle – how *old* are you?" Kayode screeched.

"Eleven." Hadim shrugged. "Now, prepare yourself." He spun his spear round in an elaborate twist.

"I think Ninki Nanka deserves a rematch," Yomi shouted from above. Everyone in the room looked up at her. Yomi had been figuring out the levers that controlled the cage. Now, wearing both Beast Hunter gloves, she pushed its metal claws in between two medium-sized cogs causing a jam. There was a squeal, screech and groan, which caused her heart to pause. Had this been a mistake? There was no point in regretting her actions now. With a mighty push Yomi put all her weight on to the glove, causing a domino effect. The gears broke down, the levers snapped and the entire cage begun to rattle.

Pling! The lock clicked open, fell to the ground and the cage door slowly creeeeeeeaaked open.

Now, there was only a resounding silence. Yomi, Kayode and Hadim stared at the cage.

Ninki Nanka gave a piercing howl and in the blink of an eye sprung through the gap to freedom.

"I am free!" he bellowed with pleasure. Finally he was able to stand in full glory and stretched his wings wide, to the full width of the dungeon.

Ninki Nanka turned his attention to Hadim. Yomi and Kayode gulped and looked at their nemesis. Even though he had raised his spear ready for battle, he didn't look so smug now. Ninki Nanka used his huge tail to slap the spear out of his hand, causing the young hunter to fall on to his bottom.

"Now *you* will make a tasty snack," Ninki Nanka said menacingly as he took one step towards Hadim.

"Wait!" shouted Kayode in alarm. "I thought you said you didn't eat humans?"

"I will make an exception for him." Ninki Nanka licked his sharp teeth.

"No, you can't." Yomi looked at Hadim.

"You wish for me to not eat him? The person who stole me from the river and the people I protect and trapped me?" Ninki Nanka stared down at Yomi and Kayode, who nodded.

Yomi might not like Hadim, but she feared what would happen if Ninki Nanka ate the son of the Beast Prime. Also, it wouldn't be right!

"Fine, as my rescuers, I will respect your wishes. But I *will* have my revenge." Ninki Nanka launched himself into the air and darted out of the dungeon, crashing through the door and surrounding wall.

Yomi and Kayode raced after the Dragon King as he flew up the stairs back to ground level. Everything except the walls were destroyed in his wake, setting free some of the trapped Nkara. He cracked Hadim's family trophies and broke all the weapons. Nothing was spared his fury.

Yomi and Kayode dodged the falling debris around them.

"I think the walls are going to cave in," Yomi yelled as they watched the Sacred Beast unleash his anger.

Behind Ninki Nanka, they saw a horrified Hadim trying to salvage the damage. "My dad is going to kill me!"

"Just tell him a dragon got loose and you didn't know what to do," Yomi offered with a smile.

Hadim scowled and pointed at her. "I swear if it's the last thing I do, I will get you both for this," he growled before his face froze. Ninki Nanka had risen up behind Yomi and Kayode but before anything else could happen another voice called out.

"HADDDDIMMMMMM!" A loud human shout vibrated through the Skyfort.

"Dad!" Hadim panicked and turning quickly back to Yomi and Kayode he hissed, "You two will pay!"

"Not today." Yomi grabbed Kayode's hand as they

climbed on top of Ninki Nanka, who swept them up into the air. The dragon then pulled back his head before releasing a powerful water blast, blowing open the front doors of the Skyfort.

Kayode grinned. "Saving dragons is fun!"

"Hold on," Ninki Nanka told them as he whizzed out of the Skyfort and into the night sky.

The bright shine of the full moon greeted them as the dragon lifted them as high as the stars. Yomi tasted the fresh air as they raced through the clouds. They put out their hands to grab it as it zoomed past them. Now this was fun – truly an *adventure*!

Ninki Nanka sprinted them back to the banks of the Gambia River and waited for Yomi and Kayode to hop down from his back.

"I thank you, Yomi and Kayode, for your help." Ninki Nanka nodded his head in a low bow of appreciation.

"No problem." Kayode gave a thumbs up to the dragon, who chuckled deeply.

"Allow me to present you with a gift of thanks. Yomi, please put out your hand." Yomi did as he instructed, and what looked like a musical instrument appeared.

"How...?" Kayode's voice trailed off in wonder.

There, in the palm of her hand, lay a small, curved horn made of dark green dragon scales. Yomi turned it around in her hands, amazed.

"Why don't you try blowing it?" Ninki Nanka suggested.

A shrill sound echoed across the river.

"It's a water horn. Consider it a gift of friendship." Ninki Nanka spread out his wings. "One day I will return this great favour you have done for me."

Slowly he lifted himself from the ground, gently circling them and the river.

"Thank you," Yomi said.

"I must warn you before I leave. The Beast Hunters' Guild is getting stronger, their hunting techniques, their use and knowledge of Yinza increasing. The Nkara are not as safe as they once were. Hadim is one, but the Guild is many." He launched himself higher into the air. "Pass on my words to the Sacred Beast League – they are the protectors of Beasts everywhere. But to be true protectors, greater measures, *risks*, must be taken to truly honour their duties."

"We will," Kayode answered.

"Goodbye!" Yomi shouted.

"I will not forget you. Thank you, both." Then he dived deep into the depths of the Gambia River.

CHAPTER 12

PUNISHMENTS AND REWARDS

Uncle Olu looked over the water horn several times, before turning back to Yomi and Kayode who were now sat at the round table of the secret 'S' room in Aunty Binta's house. Yomi continued to tell the entire S.B.L. group about Nyanya, Mustafa, Mansa's Stone, Hadim and rescuing Ninki Nanka from the dungeons of the Skyfort. Their uncle handed the horn to Aunty Binta.

"Well now, this is quite the tale," Aunty Binta said, eyeing them closely. She passed the horn down the table to Daba who, like the rest of the Sacred Beast League, couldn't keep his eyes off Yomi and Kayode. "Your niece and nephew are really quite brilliant, Olu."

"Imagine! Finding, saving and returning Ninki Nanka to safety. And they're not even members of the S.B.L.," another member called out.

"So Hadim was responsible then?" Uncle Olu said out loud. "He might not be a full Beast Hunter, but to kidnap Ninki Nanka? There has to be some kind of punishment for them."

"Yes indeed. The pact has certainly been broken," Aunty Binta declared. "I will speak with the other branches' presidents and we can collectively decide what to do." She sighed.

"And what about Yinza?" Olu asked. "You heard Ninki Nanka's warning."

"You are right," Aunty Binta muttered through a clenched jaw. She then looked down to the Beast Atlas, which Yomi explained had helped kick-start their quest. "This book belonged to my late husband." As Aunty Binta turned through the pages, Yomi couldn't tell if she was happy or sad. "He was a firm believer in Yinza magic and its uses in helping us protect and get closer to Nkara. When he died on an assignment, I wondered, how can something so dangerous, so beyond our understanding have any place in the League? Clearly, I have been proved wrong. Look at the damage a *child* was able to do." She slammed the atlas shut. "The S.B.L. cannot fall behind any further in doing our duty to protect. All right, Olu. For now, you have the full support of this branch to continue your research."

"Yes! Thank you." Uncle Olu grasped her hand with delight. "I will not let any of you down."

"Remember, be careful. We are stepping into a great unknown." The uncomfortable look on her face quickly heightened but melted away when she turned to Yomi and Kayode. "But back to these intrepid adventurers. You two have done incredibly well for your first S.B.L. mission. Even though it was unofficial."

Olu nodded in agreement. "They are amazing. Though I'm not sure how thrilled their parents will be when I tell them." His smile quickly slipped away. "So, to your punishment..."

"Punishment?!" Yomi and Kayode cried.

"Uncle Olu, we rescued the Dragon King!"

Kayode exclaimed.

"While breaking curfew! I left you both in bed but you sneaked out after I told you not to get involved," their uncle added.

"You said we did a brilliant job," Yomi jumped in.

"True," Aunty Binta agreed. "But you also disturbed Nyanya, used a sky rope to escape from my house, went to the Skyfort alone, and challenged an apprentice Beast Hunter."

Yomi looked at her brother, and Kayode looked back. "OK. What is it then?" Kayode sighed.

Aunty Binta looked to Uncle Olu for the answer.

"I will need full-time assistants for the entirety of my trip. I have a lot of places to get to, and I will need help," Olu mused.

Well, that doesn't sound so bad, Yomi thought.

"I will need help with organizing my notes, planning my talks, sorting out my reading papers..."

Kayode let out a large groan much to the amusement of the room. "*Really*, Uncle Olu?"

But Olu was not done. "I will also need help on my excavations and exploration trips."

Yomi and Kayode's eyes lit up at the mention of this. "What sort of exploration?" Yomi asked.

"We have many journeys planned which will take us all over Africa where we will definitely see more Nkara."

"I believe you two might need this." Aunty Binta handed back the Beast Atlas. "Use it well."

"Aunty." The pair smiled at the present.

"OK." Aunty Binta clapped her hands to get everyone's attention. "We should now move on to your main reward."

Yomi and Kayode swapped confused looks.

"I, Binta Ngom, wish to award Yomi and Kayode Adesina with membership to the Sacred Beast League. All in favour, say 'Waaw'."

Everyone in the room voted yes, with Uncle Olu saying it the loudest.

"Do you two wish to join?" he asked.

"Yes! Yes! Yes!" they both said at the same time. Yomi wasn't sure how their uncle would explain this to their parents but she would leave that to him.

Aunty Binta asked them both to stand up. She then revealed two gold letter 'S'-shaped brooches before pinning one to each of their T-shirts.

Yomi and Kayode high-fived each other as the room assembled to take a group photo with Kayode and Yomi at the front.

Just before the camera flashed, Yomi whispered into her brother's ear. "Forget Arabella Carter. We're going to have the best, most amazing and unforgettable adventures ever!"

ABOUT THE AUTHOR

Davina Tijani writes speculative and fantastical stories for both adults and children. She was born in London and holds degrees from University of East Anglia and University College London. She grew up on Star Wars and other science fiction, fantasy and horror films and stories. She is a huge lover of mythology and enjoys incorporating it into her writing.

🐦 @davinatijani

ABOUT THE ILLUSTRATOR

Adam Douglas-Bagley is an illustrator and storyteller from South London. Ever since he first picked up a pencil Adam has had a passion for illustrating fantastical worlds and filling them with stories. With his illustrations, Adam endeavours to explore the transportive and timeless ability of storytelling to enthral audiences. He hopes to inspire anyone with a story to tell, to pick up a pencil and share their own worlds for others to traverse.

📷 @adougiebagofdrawings

YOMI
AND THE POWER OF THE YUMBOES

Read on for a sneak peek at
Yomi's next adventure...

CHAPTER 1
THE ALL-SEEING EYE

The luminous green eye of the Beast never took its gaze off Yomi. Its deep intensity captured her and refused to let her go. She stared it down in some sort of competition. Did she dare risk it? She'd gotten away with it before, so why not once more...

Yomi gave in, unable to deny its allure, and picked up the Beast Atlas, the ultimate guide to Nkara, the powerful Beasts that roamed the African continent. She swung its metal cover open, ready to dive into its secrets. Trying to keep watch on the door too, she soon got lost in the book. Every time she read its pages, she felt the world expand a little more around her.

On the plane to Senegal, before landing in the city of Thiès, she had started reading through the guide. Now, once again braving the book's knowing, all-seeing green eye, Yomi could almost hear its warning to tread carefully if she went any further. She couldn't help but wonder if the Beast Atlas was alive. She could have sworn the eye's pupil moved back and forth as if watching her.

"Whoaaaaa!" Kayode clapped his hands, flipping through the most recent volume of Arabella Carter.

"You're supposed to be working, not reading!" Yomi pointed at him as he tried to hide behind the comic before he realized what she was doing.

"Well, you're reading the atlas!" Kayode argued.

"Fine, I'll stop. But we need to get back to the job Uncle Olu told us to do. We need to be more serious, Kay. We are members of the Sacred Beast League now."

Their uncle was a key member of the S.B.L., and worked as a Nkara researcher at the Mikosi Institute. Since joining the League they had learned about its other departments, including the Investigation Division, Beast Consultancy and Management, Science Division, and Artifact and Relic Operations, but there were more that Yomi was keen to find out about.

"We're on this trip to help Uncle with his research, which means organizing his notes before he gets back." Yomi held up the files. They had been in Senegal for two weeks now and the notes kept getting longer.

"But I've just got to the good bit. Arabella is about to enter a dormant volcano in Costa Rica," Kayode groaned, using a bookmark to save his place.

He picked up an enormous pile of papers, which had a mixture of vivid-coloured rocks on the front. "There are so many!" Kayode shuffled through the jumbled pages, putting them into order. "I don't know how Uncle is going to put all of this into one presentation."

"Uncle is the smartest guy we know, he'll figure it out," Yomi answered before sighing. "I thought now we're members, we would get to go to cool places and see loads of amazing things. All we've done is sort through paperwork! We haven't done anything. No adventures. No new Nkara."

"At least we haven't been eaten," Kayode chimed in. "I'm happy to be a S.B.L. member but I do not want to get swallowed whole."

Yomi crossed her arms. "If we get eaten, you have permission to be angry."

"It will be your fault if we do get eaten so I'll remember you said that!"